Snapper

GOULASH

GOULASH

BRIAN KIMBERLING

PANTHEON BOOKS, NEW YORK

Published in the United States by Pantheon Books,
a division of Penguin Random House LLC, New York, and
distributed in Canada by Random House of Canada,
a division of Penguin Random House Canada Limited, Toronto.

Pantheon Books and colophon are registered trademarks of Penguin Random House LLC.

Library of Congress Cataloging-in-Publication Data
Name: Kimberling, Brian, author.
Title: Goulash / Brian Kimberling.
Description: First edition. New York : Pantheon Books, 2019
Identifiers: LCCN 2018025630 | ISBN 9780307908070 (hardcover : alk. paper).
ISBN 9780307908087 (ebook).
Classification: LCC PS3611.14576 G68 2019 | DDC 813/.6—dc23 |
LC record available at lccn.loc.gov/2018025630

www.pantheonbooks.com

Jacket images: (beer) Chris Stein/Getty Images; (Old Town Hall, Prague) Vrabelpeter1/
Getty Images
Jacket design by Janet Hansen

Printed in the United States of America

First Edition

9 8 7 6 5 4 3 2 1

What can we do? It is so far from one nation to another; all of us are more and more lonely. You'd better never stick your nose out of your house again; better to lock the gate and close the shutters, and now others can wish us well as much as they like! I have finished with everyone. And now you can close your eyes and softly, quite softly, keep saying: *How do you do,* old sir in Kent? *Grüß Gott, meine Herren! Grazie, signor! À votre sante!*

—KAREL ČAPEK, *Greetings,* published December 25, 1938

PART I

ROSARY

First it was my shoes. They went missing from outside my flat, where I left them slathered in mud after a lonely late-winter walk through the countryside northwest of Prague. I bought a new pair and forgot the old until they appeared two weeks later in the window of an art gallery, as part of an installation with an asking price of over six thousand dollars, converted from Czech crowns.

At least they had been cleaned. On the other hand holes had been drilled through the soles so that they could be strung like beads with other shoes and a number of books onto a vertical rope fastened to a repurposed manhole cover on the gallery's hardwood floor and affixed at the top to the ceiling. The resulting column sagged lightly as it rose. My shoes had become part of an exotic and erudite tree. I couldn't be sure they were mine without closer examination, so I went inside.

In small print under the price tag I saw that the artist responsible for *Rosary* went only by the initials D.K. My shoes were of extravagant American provenance compared to the evidently Central and Eastern European shoes; moreover they were size 14, sensibly deployed near the bottom of the tree, and sandwiched between something in German and a military history book in English. All of the shoes and books looked used. All the major European languages were represented. The shoes were black and brown; the books red and blue and purple and orange.

At a desk in a corner sat a compact individual of indeterminate gender with shoulder-length sandy hair and a pale face, delicate hands emerging from a man's shirtsleeves splayed on the desk. I hoped they spoke English.

"Excuse me," I said. "You have my shoes in your window."

"I'm sure you're mistaken," they said, distinctly more tenor than alto.

"I'm sure I'm not," I said.

"I'm sure the artist in question steals only the shoes of other artists."

"My shoes went missing two weeks ago and now they're in your window. I can prove that they are mine."

"How do you propose to do that?"

"My name is inside them."

"And why is your name inside them?"

"My mother put it there."

He raised a lone eyebrow. I began to feel like a suspect accused of an unspecified crime.

"I see. And how old are you?"

"Twenty-three."

"This mother, she travels with you?"

"No."

"Shame. She could perhaps teach you not to insult people in European art galleries."

"It says Elliott Black on the inside tongue of each shoe. Little label she stitched in. Just have a look."

"If you wish to purchase the item you can do whatever you like with it." He seemed pained behind the comic façade, as if he had never met an American with such limited funding that a pair of shoes could be a matter of legitimate concern.

"I don't want the shoes back now. They're ruined. But I would like to know how they got here."

"You say your shoes were stolen?"

"Yes."

"I am sorry to hear it. Crime in our country is not like crime in your country."

"What does that even mean?" I said. I could also see that in his country the customer was not always right.

"I can't help you, Mr. Black. You are just visiting?"

"I teach English."

"You are a lucky man. How long have you been here?"

"About a month."

"Then you have noticed that Prague is full of statues. Where there are statues there are artists. You can't be too careful with your shoes."

"That isn't even a statue," I said.

"Would you call it a monument?"

"I'll bet those are all library books, too. I bet they have labels."

"Sadly, investigating your hypothesis would entail dismantling the object."

"How can I track down this D.K. and ask how come he stole my shoes?"

"Are artists tracked down in America? How very enlightening. Perhaps you could lure him into a trap with more shoes."

"Is there someone else I can talk to?"

He made an elaborate show of looking around. In profile he had long sideburns and an improbably long, sharp nose. He reminded me of a meerkat sentry tasting the wind.

"I see no one."

I looked around, too. The gallery also contained a working pram made from papier-mâché pornography, a large wax bust of Lenin laughing, and several glass articles of no obvious appeal or utility. The remaining space was devoted to paintings.

"If you would like to complain to the manager," he said, "I am listening."

"You have to admit that I have a mystery here," I said.

"Are your shoes comfortable?"

"What?"

"The ones you are wearing."

"I suppose."

"The square toe suits you," he said. "I generally think of Americans as sneaker people."

"Oh, come on," I said. "Cowboy boots."

"Touché," he said.

"Do you have a name?" I said.

"Certainly, Mr. Black. I am Mr. Cimarron."

"Well, Mr. Cimarron, if you would tell Mr. D.K. that Mr. Black is annoyed I'd appreciate it."

"I do not actually know that D.K. is a man," he said. "My assistant handles weekend deliveries. Perhaps I infer it from the phallic nature of the work. Would you call it furniture?"

"I would call it my shoes."

"The way it droops as it rises does suggest some performance anxiety, don't you think?"

I was compelled to look at it again. Every shoe was polished and every book spine uncracked; I could almost imagine somebody wanting it at the end of the sofa in a living room somewhere. Around it instead were gleaming floorboards, immaculate walls, a spotless window; outside young men and women in sportswear laughing, cars honking, history erased and replaced by this absurd artifact with no immediate meaning that I could detect.

"I prefer to think of it as a tree," I said.

"A tree with performance anxiety. Your ideas are fascinating. Would you call it an entity?"

"I'd be dazzled if anyone created a thing that isn't an entity."

"Yet we can create entities that are not things."

"I suppose."

"Or can we? You're the English teacher."

"Fine," I said. "The rain is a thing that falls on the plain, mainly, also a thing, of Spain, which is more of an entity."

"You illustrate my point beautifully. Poor Spain can't fall on anything."

"That doesn't strike me as a point. And the plain is going to have trouble with that, too."

"Is a point an entity or a thing?"

"Yes."

We glared at each other.

"I don't suppose you want to tell me the point of the thing," I said, pointing at it.

He shrugged.

"To make money, of course."

WILD WEST

My flat was on a tram-addled boulevard opposite shops with windows tricked out in funky and dignified words I couldn't read or pronounce. Cimarron's art gallery was about two tram stops away. Otherwise there wasn't anything artsy to my eye about the neighborhood. It was stuck in the past like the rest of the country, with identical menus in every restaurant, posters of footballers dated 1984 in every pub, and men in ancient dungarees operating forklifts on the sidewalks. Things had changed in the city center with the influx of Western tourists and cash—Prague and Warsaw were competing to see who could build the first moneymaking museum of communism—but I lived in an outpost of stagnation, beneath a charming and oppressive air of Slavic mystery.

The next morning on my way to teach I saw a pair of stone

legs and sandaled feet sticking out of a metal garbage can. Closer inspection suggested someone had dismantled a statue with a sledgehammer. *Stone* wasn't the word—it was some form of concrete with bits of thick wire armature protruding from each severed limb. A woman's head with half a nose lay between the thighs at the bottom of the can, a forearm and hand propped up against that. An adjacent can contained her torso, and the other arm. Both cans held a depth of rubble and dust.

A corrugated metal shutter covered in graffiti was the only clue that there was a studio from which she had come. Everything else in the area was resolutely residential: curtained windows and door-side ranks of buttons for flats one through forty. I stood still, watching people for a while. I saw a lanky boy carrying his football, and a manifestly bored mother dragging her toddler around, two elderly gentlemen out for a morning stumble, and, finally, the trash collectors, who slung the dismembered figure unceremoniously and without comment into the back of their truck.

I had become attuned to the sounds of my neighborhood. Any tapping, buzzing, blasting noise suggested someone somewhere hard at work, but before I could figure out where exactly, another tram clattered by, drowning out all other noise. Yet visual evidence came and went like signs of spring. A life-sized wooden bear evidently carved with a chainsaw stood outside the grocery store for two days, then vanished. Small bicycles made from twisted wire coat hangers appeared dangling from street signs and traffic lights. The shop window of an antiques store featured an enormous desk spangled with spoons and keys. Twice I saw a small marble obelisk strapped to the roof of a car.

·   ·   ·

I taught about half my lessons in a pub over beer and cigarettes, writing American slang on napkins. It was incredibly demoralizing. I had worked hard and paid well for my teaching certification. I had imagined working with motivated students and being a good ambassador for my country, as my mother put it, by which she meant say "please" and "thank you." Instead I got bored midlevel insurance executives who just wanted to chat. English lessons were tedious company policy, and attendance was correspondingly poor. For a given class only one or two students bothered to show. Meanwhile the full might and majesty of the American legal system was conducting DNA tests on a blue dress from the Gap. My students' curiosity on the subject was excruciating, particularly if I had prepared a lesson on, say, reported speech, but they peppered me with questions instead.

Teaching English felt mostly like leading parlor games at children's parties, except my students weren't children, paid little attention, and got virtually nothing out of the experience. I would ask them, for example, to write, "I am not a nice person," followed by three to five sentences illustrating the thesis. Then I would ask them to swap pronouns on the fly ("You are not a nice person, and here's why . . ."). It was a good exercise for subject-verb agreement, and I enjoyed the way we seemed to be flipping verbal rocks to see what lived under them. The benefit for my students was spending an hour away from a spreadsheet, and not much more.

Ivan Biskup came consistently, which surprised me as he was senior among them and thus presumably busy. Milan Jezdec and Vlasta Havran were the other two most constant. Milan was athletic and in his midthirties with a seemingly terminal case of ennui. He told me early on that when he was not on a tennis court he was bored. Vlasta was very diffident and drank only half pints. Her hair was amorphous, wiry, and a shade of brown closest to dark grey. Her nose had been broken in a car accident and never set itself right afterward. In a bad mood she looked like an extra from some documentary film about the horrors of totalitarianism, yet when she smiled she was strikingly lovely.

In any case, Ivan could authorize lessons in the Golden Lion. This particular pub's décor was still a thoroughly drab arrangement for an oppressed people, a place for communist commiseration rather than capitalist celebration. The tables and chairs were on their last legs, and the walls decorated strictly with nicotine. Still, it was preferable to an empty boardroom, and an essential component, Ivan said, of my own intercultural education. Czech history and culture, he added, are best appreciated in a pint glass.

Ivan explained local idiosyncrasies to me, like the way Czech men enter buildings before their female companions "in case there's a fight," which suggested to me that I had in fact moved to the Wild West. He also hazarded a guess about the shattered statue: that if three or four Prague artists lived in close proximity they doubtless spent most of their time and energy sabotaging each other's work and framing the other guy.

We had installed ourselves once I arrived over a red-and-white checkered tablecloth, and when the waitress appeared I tried out my Czech. She was petite, blonde, very pretty, and about eighteen. She turned as red as the tablecloth checkers and ran away. Ivan slapped his thigh.

"I know what you were trying to say," he said. "It just sounded like *I think you know what I want, baby.*"

She did return with my Czech beer of choice. I had only been there six weeks. The beer was Velkopopovický Kozel, which

Ivan translated as "the Goat from Greater Popovitz." Weak and slightly metallic, it was perfect for daytime drinking.

I told my students about the legs.

"You are a lucky man," they said.

Living in Žižkov was like living in Brooklyn, they told me. I wondered what pirated movies their conception of Brooklyn came from, and I privately thought the comparison more aspirational than accurate. Žižkov was either very working class or very Bohemian or both, with a reputation for spontaneous brawling. Also, unlike Brooklyn, Žižkov was named after a one-eyed mace-wielding general who 575 years previously had slaughtered hundreds of Catholics in nearby Kutná Hora and hurled their corpses into the local silver mines. The statue of him on a hill in the middle of Žižkov was the best-endowed equestrian statue in the world.

Ivan mentioned a major sculpture contest or contests upcoming. Thanks to communism there were all sorts of horrible things to commemorate. A major exhibition was scheduled in a Žižkov park. Prague's finest would contribute their best. We made plans to go.

Meanwhile to satisfy my curiosity about D.K., I thought perhaps I should duck into some art galleries. My interest in visual art did not usually extend beyond Daffy Duck.

I looked into other galleries full of inscrutable items—dead bees in small lightbulbs arranged to spell GUILE in English, screen-printed close-ups of fingers, lips, and cigarettes, and a whole photography exhibition called Forty-Two Breakfasts in Dresden, in which all the photos were taken after the breakfasts had been eaten. I found no further trace of D.K. I still wanted restitution for my shoes: money, an explanation, some form of shoe justice. Eventually I returned to the first gallery to find an altogether different man at the desk, an older man in jeans and a jacket with no tie. His mustache looked laser trimmed. I explained that I had visited once before, when I spoke to Mr. Cimarron.

I could see from his face that I had just told him a fantastic joke.

"Oh, you did?"

"I did."

"What did he look like?"

"You would know that since he claimed to be the manager."

"I am the manager," he said.

"Great," I said. "I came in to ask how my shoes came to be part of that thing in the window. Mr. Cimarron was very evasive."

"Mr. Cimarron sat where I sit now?"

"Yes."

"What day was this?"

"I don't know. Two weeks ago, maybe."

"Your shoes are almost certainly part of the thing because Mr. Cimarron put them there."

"Mr. Cimarron and the artist D.K. are the same," I suggested. My mystery was simply a prank.

"Oh, no," he said. "Cimarron is not a name in Czech, but Mr. Cimrman is a great Czech hero. There is an asteroid named after him between Mars and Jupiter."

Over the next few days the park filled with crates and tarpaulin-shrouded lumps; an invisible brigade of sculptors had clearly unloaded, installed, covered, and padlocked dozens of striking novelties. Two men in private security uniforms patrolled. The effect was exactly as though a secret playground lay under the tarps and children were absolutely prohibited from having any fun there. I tried to guess from sizes and shapes, and I looked for a loose tarp that I could peer under without attracting attention. While under wraps it was the most intriguing exhibition in the world. After nightfall it resembled a graveyard, plastic headstones gleaming in the moonlight. Scattered trees stood guard to keep down the jealous dead.

Eventually I dutifully scaled Vítkov Hill, past charming stone walls afflicted with the new Western scourge of graffiti, to see the great national monument. It's true: Jan Žižka rides a monster horse.

GOOD SOLDIER

Saturday morning, 10:00 a.m., Ivan knocked on my door. He wore shorts and a T-shirt and brought beer, which we opened.

"This is it? This is your whole flat?"

I had a single room adjacent to the landlady's, with whom I shared a bathroom and a hallway lined with the sort of cooking equipment I associated with camping expeditions. As far as I knew these were standard Czech living arrangements. I did have—through a vast window—a good view of the monstrous space-age architectural experiment alleged to be the Prague TV tower, and I got plenty of sunlight when there was any. Once a week the landlady cleaned and left a dry, inedible pastry for me. I had to dispose of it elsewhere since she also emptied the trash.

"This is it," I said.

"It has great location," he said. "Great location."

"Brooklyn, I'm told."

"I don't know what you'd do with a TV anyway," he said. "Maybe learn Czech."

I sat on the edge of my threadbare red communist sofa, which folded out into half a bed full of springs, spikes, and needles. He sat in my one rickety wooden chair and looked worried my table might not take the weight of his beer.

"Some advice, though," he said. "If you meet a nice girl, go to her place."

Such advice was not covered in the teaching abroad handbook.

I filled Ivan in on the disappointing solution to my mystery. Ivan said that he could have spared me some embarrassment had I told him the story of the shoe thief earlier. Jára Cimrman was a fictional Czech entity who showed Thomas Edison how to change a lightbulb, personally fertilized Chekhov's cherry orchard, and accomplished many other laudable things. He once missed the North Pole by just twenty-three feet, and instructed Mendeleev to remove the element of surprise. He scribbled some notes while Darwin sailed the *Beagle,* and later he loaned some money to Mr. Dunlop to develop his pneumatic tire. He was a philosopher, playwright, inventor, musician, advisor to American presidents, and more.

"Possibly," said Ivan, "the grandfather of one Robert Zimmerman from Hibbing, Minnesota."

"Not my quarry then."

"What's quarry?"

"Something you want to turn into dinner."

"Remind me which state you are from?" said Ivan. "I know it begins with an *I*."

"That gives you Idaho, Iowa, Illinois, and Indiana. Indiana

is the state that takes longest to drive through, psychologically. Roads that never end or bend. Dead flat."

"Not to mention the people," said Ivan.

"Quite."

"In school we all learned to use a watch as a compass so we could hide in the woods when the Americans came," he said.

"We hid under our desks to prepare for you guys dropping bombs."

"Wow," he said. "Either you had a low opinion of our bombs or a high opinion of your desks. Sorry. We're just very aware of being a faraway country of which you know nothing, as Neville Chamberlain called us shortly after authorizing our destruction. How long do you think you'll stay?"

"The idea is to burnish a grad school application with teaching experience," I said. "I don't know."

"Why burn an application?"

"*Burnish* is more like shine than burn."

"In which subject?"

"History."

"No offense, but does anyone in America just go get a job? Or is that a kind of barbarian practice you've evolved through?"

There were thirty thousand of us in Prague at the time, either teaching English or living off trust funds. I had, if I got into trouble, the Bank of Mom.

"What do your parents do?"

"Well, they're divorced. My mom is the sort of seemingly easygoing librarian who keeps things exactly in order. My dad is a philosophy professor and a complete mess."

"Librarian is kind of a job," he said.

"I assume there was no such thing as private insurance under communism," I said. I didn't know how Ivan or anyone else had become qualified for their new capitalist jobs. "What did you do before?"

"I was a soldier," he said. "Sort of. I did my national service and stayed on afterward, but I mostly sat at a desk doing risk evaluation. Much the same as I do now but in a different context. If we have fifty helicopters that explode twenty-five percent of the time, how many pilots are we going to go through before we can get a mission done?"

"And now?"

"I determine who is at fault in horrible industrial accidents," he said. "Beer helps."

He told me at length about gruesome transactions between heavy machinery and human hands and feet. It was unclear why Ivan was required to take English lessons, particularly since he had spent six months attached to a Massachusetts emergency clinic while completing a dissertation on necrosis. I suspected that he liked English lessons as a way of avoiding the ceaseless pain and misery pervading every aspect of his job, and his complicity in keeping intact the system that tolerated it.

Ivan's hair was glaringly orange, but it was receding tragically, too. He appeared to have received instructions to proceed straight to middle age. Powerful shoulders and arms were offset by a paunch that refused to comply with his shirts. He shifted positions often with a wince at whichever joint was troubling him at the moment. His blue eyes were both pale and piercing, but his long, pointed nose and downturned mouth gave him the look of a puzzled, avuncular fox.

"There are three prizes today," he told me. "I looked into it. The first is in reproductions. Everything original must be replaced eventually. Someday the Charles Bridge and all its statues will all secretly live in a big American warehouse with the

Ark of the Covenant. The winner or winners of that contest will be in work for life. The communists didn't care about statues. All kinds of arms and legs and heads need to be fixed or fitted around Prague."

I imagined a vast stew of stone body parts.

"The second thing I had to look up in English. Memorials. This one is potentially controversial since most of us would just like to forget those forty-one and a half years. But it's open-ended. Anything can be memorized."

"Memorialized."

"Yes."

"Commemorated is even better."

"OK. It's Saturday."

"I know."

"The winner of that prize will probably get to show tourists how we suffered at places like Prague Castle and Wenceslas Square."

"I should enter my sofa for it."

"I had one just like it. I took it out to the country cottage and gave it new life as firewood." He paused thoughtfully. "After the revolution I bought a second freezer so I could put a whole cow in it. Meat was that cheap. We had been sending all of ours east. The third category is the open-ended contest with a sort of note about future. We can't just be this backward people looking backward at all times."

"I don't know," I said. "The American South manages that fairly well."

"Can you teach me to speak with a twang?"

"Just give every syllable an extra syllable."

We practiced for a while until his English was perfectly unintelligible.

The sound of a brass band reached us from the park three streets away, so we finished our beers and made our move.

The park was ringed by beer vendors and sausage stands. The band played on a tented stage beneath the television tower while a few hundred men, women, and children ignored them. The new sculptures were still covered but they had attendants. I could see for the first time that they formed three groups, but I was distracted. There were creepy giant bronze babies scaling the TV tower. From their vantage all of Prague's roof cover was laid out like a terra-cotta tarpaulin over strange undulations, punctuated by a hundred spires.

The band stopped and a man in a pale blue linen suit spoke ceremonial Czech for ten minutes. It was indistinguishable from any other variety of Czech. He raised an arm and signaled that the work should be unveiled.

The reconstructions area was populated almost entirely by gargoyles of every size, kind, and material: demons, dragons, leopards, and fish all glaring at each other with otherworldly contempt. Some of them were fanciful hybrids of reptile and mammal or mammal and mineral. Ivan observed that all of them were functional waterspouts.

In memorials we found a female figure identical to the one I had seen in the garbage can, except she had been chipped and battered tastefully so that her torso and her dignity remained intact. A small card indicated that she was fashioned from Cimint Fondu.

We came in the future section to a life-sized and realistic female nude in wood, except that through a cutaway from behind you could see she had a miniature bedroom in her left breast and a kitchen in her right. Where her womb should have been several miniature men were comparing tennis rackets next to a well-stocked bar.

Next to her stood Mr. Cimarron. I tried to think up an appropriate query about my shoes, or even decide how to address him. He stood smiling at me. Until suddenly he wasn't.

He tackled me with an effeminate but effective shoulder to the gut, so I was already on the grass gazing skyward when something swung audibly in an arc through the air over my head. Mr. Cimarron rolled away, and looking farther back, I saw Ivan, upside down, exercising his combat training against a large blond man wielding a broken pool cue. This netted Ivan a fist on the cheek from one of the man's confederates, who was duly tackled by Mr. Cimarron. Mr. Cimarron was then hauled from the ground by a fifth pair of hands, but the testicles corresponding to those hands were mashed by a sixth knee. Ivan, as far as I could tell, was enjoying himself, but I thought I should at least stand up. I was enveloped in a cloud of knuckles and boots.

Time dilated. A gnarly thing like an arm approached my head, but I somehow dodged, and it went off in search of an easier target. My chest met lots of elbows. Several clouts I did receive were not intended for me. The air was thick with the battle snort of the Slavic warrior.

Articles of black clothing materialized among us, and bright badges flashed as black sleeves began swinging. Black truncheons were applied to the insides of knees, causing the proprietors of the knees to drop instantly. The inhabiters of the black clothing destroyed the festive and fraternal spirit of the thing.

The Czech language has a special disdain for vowels, even or especially when it is being shouted angrily by fifteen or twenty men simultaneously. The lips of the shouters do not open wide and their faces are not operatic. I couldn't understand what was said but felt as we all lay bruised in the grass that we were having a very stressed-out picnic. I found myself next to Mr. Cimarron with just a pair of police boots and their standing occupant separating us.

"What the hell?" I said.

"Sometimes," he said, "an artist doesn't just steal shoes, but the wives of other artists, too."

"Well, that sounds traditional," I said. "Why did you tackle me?"

"I saw them coming. I thought it best for your safety if we did not appear to be friends."

"I think I could have explained that."

"They were not in a listening mood. Your friend was most helpful," he added. "Thanks to him I should have only two black eyes. You don't look terrible."

"Thanks. Where is the wife in question?"

"I don't know. I don't really steal them. I borrow them. In pairs. Also traditional."

Abruptly, Mr. Cimarron and the man with the pool cue were singled out for questioning and taken aside. The rest of us were permitted to go.

Something was awry. The assembled crowd wasn't looking at us.

Ivan helped me up with a red hand, and around us we found a scene of beautiful carnage: by accident or design, the line of gargoyles on plinths had toppled like dominoes, crashing ultimately into the stone woman and breaking her all over again. The work was much better than anything that could be made on purpose—very lifelike, the way the fish chipped a tooth on the leopard while the dragon stuck a wing in the giraffe's ear, and the woman was ambushed by a whole army of fantastical creatures while she looked the other way.

TRUST

Despite my getting him in a fight, Ivan came to the next class. It was a sunny gathering. Milan and Vlasta were discussing something in Czech, which I strongly discouraged unless it was of vital importance. Finally Ivan nodded and turned to face me.

"We watch a lot of American movies," he said. "We have noticed that there are many more black asses than white asses. Not visually. In speech."

"Get your black ass in here," said Milan. I had never heard it in a Central European monotone. The Golden Lion, which had been serving beer since 1499, probably hadn't heard it either.

I suspected Milan was a ladies' man, because he dressed the part with a collection of special boots, rode a motorcycle, and didn't talk much, just sat there square jawed and squinty, waiting to be free to do something else.

"In Czech everyone has an ass," said Vlasta.

"Like life," said Ivan.

My training was woefully inadequate.

"In America," I said, "a black ass is a badge of honor, while a white ass is more of a liability."

"So how do we say it?" said Vlasta.

"Well, I just wouldn't. I don't think you'll need it for insurance purposes." All of them worked in insurance.

"Also," said Ivan, "we don't understand *ass* as an adjective. Vlasta heard something about an ass spider on TV last night. Milan and me have heard similar things."

"Are you sure it wasn't a big-ass spider?"

"It may have been," said Vlasta.

I fished for pen and paper, sensing that a napkin was inadequate for the task at hand.

BIG-ASS SPIDER
SLOW-ASS TRAIN
GREEDY-ASS POLITICIAN

"The hyphens are optional," I said. "And historically I suppose it was *assed*." I wrote that down, too. "The spider had a very large ass, and even the politician's ass was greedy for money or power. Now it's just a standard part of colloquial American speech. I guess. Tacked on."

"My dirty-ass dog," said Ivan.

"That's perfect," I said, "but a bit literal. As if you are talking about the dog's ass, not the dirty dog." I kept my voice down in view of the subject matter, but my students spoke at a normal volume, as they were simply learning a new language.

"But the ass for a dog," said Ivan, "all trust begins there."

"True. But you can't trust the American use of *ass,* because *badass* means excellent."

"Can an ass be good?" asked Vlasta.

"Well, it can, but it's unusual. This is some good-ass beer, I suppose."

"I don't typically want my beer to have an ass," said Ivan.

"But Milan is a badass, not a good ass, on the tennis court," I said. Milan was obsessive, often playing or practicing on his lunch hour. Often he doodled during lessons, and at a glance I thought he was doing some kind of freestyle geometry. When I finally asked what he was drawing it turned out to be endless exercises in Euclidean tennis, calculating the range of possible returns from a given position on the court, juxtaposing angles and contrasting parabolas to gauge the likelihood of scoring.

"Thank you," said Milan.

"Moreover, a smart-ass is a bad thing," I said.

"I'm very confused," said Milan. "I want to ask if there are other bad asses, but you just told us bad asses are good."

"A wise-ass is also bad," I said.

"How can that be?"

"It thinks itself superior," I said.

"It's very like communism," said Ivan. "The workers are good. The professions are bad. Things mean the reverse of what they mean."

"Truth is in dogs," said Vlasta.

"The new regime is the same as the old," said Milan.

"Hard to disagree about dogs," I said.

"I do not understand," said Vlasta, "how a bad ass can be good."

"The corruption of the system runs that deep," said Ivan.

"If you see an ass that is actually bad you have no way to describe it," said Milan.

"You can say that it's a terrible ass," I said, "but that wouldn't be very polite."

"The manners of the bourgeoisie have perverted the very language," said Ivan.

"Can I use it to describe things that are just okay?" said Vlasta.

"Not really," I said.

"So how good or bad must a thing be to have an ass?" she asked.

"Think of it as comparatives and superlatives. Big, bigger, biggest, big-ass, biggest-ass."

"Verbal hyperinflation," said Milan.

"You won't need this for insurance, either," I said. "But for understanding American movies it might help."

With my black ballpoint pen on the same sheet of paper I wrote:

FUCKING BIG-ASS SPIDER
FUCKING SLOW-ASS TRAIN
FUCKING GREEDY-ASS FUCKING POLITICIAN

"It's used indiscriminately for emphasis, more so coastally than where I am from," I said.

"What part of speech is this, technically?" said Milan.

"I'm not sure. Meaningless modifier. Historically I can only speculate. It's common where I'm from to drop the final *g*."

"I fuck like my bicycle," said Ivan.

Fearing an outbreak of ill-considered usage, I ran some drills. They spoke every word with equal emphasis, which was maddening to listen to. They became increasingly vexed and perplexed. Milan wanted to know if the word was a gerund. I had to encourage them all not to run around saying *I like the fucking*. Vlasta lost it.

"We want to know which rules we can break," she said. "In Czech, it's easy. None."

"You people," said Ivan. "You make rules for the express purpose of breaking them. Speed limit fifty-five? Absurd. Drinking age twenty-one? Ridiculous. Now you are telling us we can use a word to mean anything except what it means."

Their sincere interest was heartbreaking, and I felt that I was doing a terrible job of teaching them the wrong things. I heard my voice cracking, and Vlasta put an arm on my sleeve and asked what was wrong. I said that clearly that famous fucking iron curtain was made of muslin.

Ivan earned an A+.

"You're kind of a sensitive plant, Elliott," he said. "There was also a famous fucking wall."

GOULASH

I walked home from the Golden Lion feeling frustrated and jaded, in particular because I knew that all my friends in America were shoving numbers around on screens in office cubicles, and I should be content drinking beer for pay in excellent company. Yet I also felt that I had gone from a standard American student lifestyle to something even looser, less purposeful, and less meaningful. The next step was sea sponge. Other expats I knew all styled themselves writers, but their chief ambition was manifestly matching Hemingway's alcohol consumption. Aside from downing absinthe in the *literární kavárna,* I didn't know where to go, what to do, or who to hang out with. I was homesick. I had imagined myself as a sort of fearless Jesuit bringing compassion and enlightenment to the downtrodden; reality consisted of hangovers and conjugation exercises. An old roommate, Marty, was doing missionary work for real, teaching kids and living on the South Side of Chicago, where he had learned to distinguish firearms by the sounds they made, like birdsong.

I passed my shoes, still in the gallery window mingling with Marx and Nietzsche. After ten minutes' further walking, I saw plumes of cigarette smoke unfurling from the open metal shutter near the garbage cans where I had seen the first shattered statue. The smoker of the cigarette may have identified me before I identified him. He did not seem at all surprised to see me.

"Good evening, Mr. Black."

"You're not in jail," I said. I was delighted to see him for some reason, possibly that he was the only person in Prague I knew who was not my student.

"In our country only good men go to jail," he said.

"Do you have a real name?"

"I have several. I'm sure you do, too."

"Do you have a job?"

He shrugged.

"Bricolage, mostly," he said. "I am a bricoleur. A bricologiste. A brick."

"Well, Brick, my first name is Elliott."

"I see. Have you had dinner?"

"No."

"Perhaps you will join me after I have cleaned up." He flicked his filter into the street and turned into the small studio. I couldn't see anything he was working on, just an enormous assortment of bags and buckets, some flimsy tables and sturdy sawhorses, and a lot of newspapers. Scattered around like toys lay numerous hammers, brushes, and chisels. I asked if he had been responsible for the shattered woman.

Cimarron in a dusty thick apron over T-shirt and jeans was

at once more and less androgynous than he had first seemed: muscular yet svelte, graceful but strong. I thought he could probably perpetrate the look he wanted on a given day yet pass through a crowd unnoticed if he liked.

"No," he said, "that was a friend." He rolled down the shutter and knelt to fasten it with a padlock. Standing, he put an arm on my shoulder.

"I sold the work you objected to. I am buying. Come."

We began walking.

"Who bought it?"

"A Frenchman of limited intelligence," he said. He did not sound very pleased. He pushed at a door two doors along revealing, miraculously, a pub, dark and greasy. Long tables ran the length of the room as if it were a prison mess hall—designed for quick and efficient service of a large population of drinkers. There were not many other customers, though. We took the end of one trestle table. The waitress was with us before we were finished sitting down.

"Can you read a Czech menu?" he said.

"More or less," I said.

I knew that blocks of deep-fried cheese called *smažený sýr* were safe. I hadn't ventured much further afield. Czech fries were always better than the fries of other nations, perhaps because they were required to be commensurate with the beer. For other Czech foods in my experience, taste and nutritional value appeared to be afterthoughts.

"Is there a difference," I said, "between Czech goulash and Hungarian goulash?"

"Both consist of things that don't belong together," he said.

"That doesn't sound very appetizing," I said.

"The subject most dear to my heart," he said.

"Bricolage," I said.

"But much more. Look where we are. East meets West. Communism meets capitalism. Boys meet girls. All tragic arrangements."

"We can't really un-invent any of those things," I said.

"If they exist," he said, "as things or entities."

"Is the goulash here good?" I said.

"Czech onions are very reliable," he said. "The bell peppers are probably imported. The meat varies and may be imported, too. Perhaps less so since the revolution. Same for the other ingredients."

"Are you going to answer my question?"

"I have. Czech goulash does not exist. As a thing although possibly as an entity. Therefore I can't tell you whether it is any good."

"Do we agree that beer exists?" I said.

"I will agree to that when it arrives," he said.

I asked for a Velkopopovický Kozel. He asked for the same.

"What's *prsíčka?*" I said, pointing at the menu.

"Tits of the chicken," he said.

"Breast."

"Ah, yes. I do know that. I spent time in London."

"Doing what?"

"I don't remember."

"I don't believe that."

"Learning to taste different metals through my fingertips," he said. "That is how I remember it."

"You can do that, but you can't tell me about the goulash?"

The waitress set our beers down and commenced waiting again.

"It's chili invented by desperate Hungarian cowboys," he said.

"So the Czech version is like the Hungarian version," I said.

"Neither exists," he said.

"They exist in menus and cookbooks and labels or categories for selling things," I said.

"They do."

"And you told me during our first encounter that the purpose of your work was to make money."

"I did?"

"Logically you can't stand outside the system questioning its existence while using its proceeds to buy me dinner."

"Unexpectedly right-wing of you, Elliott."

"Shall I order the right wing of the chicken?"

"That is a great business model," he said. "Food for purists."

"Then I should order the goulash," I said.

"That is an acceptance of fate," he said.

"I typically go with the deep-fried cheese," I said.

"That shows a lack of courage and a failure of imagination," he said. "Also, never trust a vegetarian."

"What are you having?"

"I haven't thought about it yet," he said.

He appeared to contemplate the chicken breast of conviction, the goulash of resignation, and the fried cheese of constipation.

"It is possible we should have gone somewhere else," he said, before asking the waitress for more beers.

"How does one taste metal through one's fingertips?"

"It is like perfect pitch. First you must have the gift and second you must practice."

"But unlike perfect pitch it has no use," I suggested.

"*Use* is not the word I would use."

"Are you going to tell me your name?"

"No. Are you going to order your food?"

The waitress had gone to take somebody else's order.

"The waitress doesn't exist," I said.

.　　.　　.

I tried the next morning to remember further inanities, or whether he had told me anything meaningful. I did remember that both of us ordered goulash, but otherwise my memory was wiped clean by alcohol. I woke on the sofa still dressed with a throbbing headache and feeling like a form of large vermin. In my jacket pocket I found a crumpled napkin with a phone number beneath the words *when you need help*. I wonder what I had divulged to him. Anyway, I still wouldn't know who to ask for.

KITTEN HEADS

Later that day I was introduced to Amanda Smith beneath the astronomical clock. She was a new recruit from Britain, phenomenally good-looking, and another teacher named Jayne whom I knew slightly was showing her around town. We were formally made acquainted.

"What happened to your eye?" she said.

"I just live in a really dangerous neighborhood," I said. "It's like living in the Bronx."

"I've been to New York," she said.

"I haven't."

"I had duck a l'orange on top of the World Trade Center," she said.

"I've never had duck a l'orange either," I said.

"Where in the States are you from?"

"Indiana."

"Oh, is that a real place?"

"Good question. It might be the only real place. It's like the South's middle finger. Which corner of Britain are you from?"

"Somerset."

"What do you know?" I said. "I've never been there either. I lived in Lincolnshire when I was ten though."

Her abundant blond hair was tied back from her face with two strands from the front. Her face was as wholesome as an apple, and her hazel eyes were tinged with orange. She wore the sort of turquoise jacket bought in a shop nobody else knows about, and under a long tight black skirt she had hips and thighs that looked ready to go bounding across the savannah. She wore sturdy brown English boots.

"Where else have you never been?" she said.

The clock stopped.

"Alphabetically? That could take a while."

"I have time."

"My passport is fairly empty," I said.

"You're young."

We looked at the clock. For six hundred years the sun has dawdled across the clock face while the moon swings around and a large zodiac rolls the other way, casting an ominous shadow over the pale blue background panel representing daylight. The clock face is flanked by carved figures—to the left, Vanity regards a mirror, while a miser guards his gold; to the right, a half-dressed skeleton who strikes the hour stands with a bearded Turk playing a lute or at least an instrument with four strings and a scrolled neck. *Clock* is an inadequate word for it; it's a planetarium and an astrolabe and a music box: serious town square bling. I could never work out the time from it, and I never met anyone who could.

We had already turned Jayne into a third wheel. Showing new teachers the sights was okay, but represented an unpaid use of a Saturday, and it looked as though the ladies were not going to make friends due to some uncanny ability among the British to divine the other's origin and socioeconomic stratum by accent alone. Jayne suggested that since I was clearly up to no good, perhaps I might show Amanda around that day, and Amanda might keep me out of trouble.

Our first stop was some Allied bomb damage on the city hall—one of very few scars left by the war. I explained that Czechs were very proud of their pacifism, to the great annoyance of the Polish. I told her that cobblestones are called "kitten heads" in Czech, and we commenced the first of many walks. I asked what had brought her to Prague.

"I just aspire to something other than a mortgage," she said.

"Are mortgages compulsory in Britain?"

"Just mammoth debt."

"What other things besides mortgages are there?"

"Is this a list you'd like by Tuesday?"

"Is contemporary art on it?"

"In what sense?"

"Not acquiring it. Giggling at it."

"Oh, certainly."

"I could show you some outstandingly ridiculous things," I said.

"We just met," she said.

"Where do you live?" I said.

"Oh, God," she said. "Doom."

Hotel Dům was a notorious rectilineal excrescence in the

communist outskirts. The top three floors were all occupied by oddball English teachers. The building was visible from nearly anywhere, like a tombstone for human promise and ambition.

"You should have seen last night's dinner," she said. "I think it was meat from a meat farm where they grow meat. Three eyes, two tails, whatever."

"Deep-fried cheese is usually safe," I said.

"I have a Canadian roommate," she said. "And she has about five posters of Siouxsie Sioux staring menacingly at my bed."

"Can you retaliate? We could go poster shopping."

"I'd rather avoid an arms race. I don't really care about the posters, but she's nuts."

"Bit worried about you," I said.

"Oh, the other residents of Doom are much worse. There is this Matterhorn of recycling in the communal kitchen. And the kitchen tap spouts human hair."

"How long have you been here?" I said.

"Four days."

"Well," I said. "It just gets weirder."

"In my copy of *The Good Soldier Švejk*," she said, "the translator's note says that justice can't be done to Czech profanity using only the hackneyed obscenities available in English."

"Wow," I said. "The world's filthiest tongue. That's some compliment."

We talked about books. She leaned heavily toward contemporary British domestic fiction, which set off a whole train of paralyzing speculation: what if she preferred tea to coffee? That could compromise all my own domestic fantasies, which also involved jazz, newspapers, and scrambled eggs on Sunday mornings. What if she took milk and/or sugar in her tea or her coffee? How many hours of my life would I lose servicing that preference over the next seven decades? Would our children play by themselves? Would I appear in fresh flannel at the top of the staircase when the guests arrived for dinner even though I had spent all afternoon sinking fence posts shirtlessly in the summer sun? I missed the names of her favorite authors.

She asked what I liked and I admitted that I had read every book Louis L'Amour ever wrote—a form of rebellion, since they were all available at the library, and in my dad's collection *Being and Nothingness* had mated with *Being and Time* with predictable results.

We talked about money. The Czech government was always a day away from collapse, Ivan had told me, and political and economic crises and scandals, along with corruption, fraud, and skullduggery, kept the Czech crown in freefall all year— fantastic news for anyone with a British or American bank card. Everything got cheaper and cheaper. When the crown shed ten percent in a single day all the foreigners rushed out to buy new sofas and holidays in Japan. Amanda said that perhaps profiting gleefully from the suffering of millions of people was not a good look. I didn't have a rebuttal for that, and we weren't ready to start talking about real estate yet. I dug the smallest of Czech coins, the heller, from my pocket and bet her that I could make it float on top of a pint of beer.

After a couple of drinks she let her hair down over her face and looked just like Chewbacca. I hoped we could have the sort of living room where the TV is not a combination of altar and eyeball. The sofa on which I rubbed her weary feet should be purple or orange. Sadly I would be compelled to watch *Raise the Red Lantern.*

On a napkin I scribbled some Czech phrases and we prac- ticed saying *ř,* a combination of *r, z, s,* and *h,* as in Dvořák. It was like a strange mating ritual between hostile proto-literates. Both of us, fond of vowels, said *urge*. Czech is a spiky language orthographically, and it sounds like some intricate artillery being primed. *"Strc prst skrz krk"* is a vowel-less sentence meaning "stick your finger through your neck"—it is illustrative, and onomatopoeic, and, at half speed, exactly what Clint Eastwood's gun says when he is about to deliver a memorable line. Yet when Amanda spoke Czech she sounded like some great Slavic goddess who was more generous toward men than were the deities of other cultures.

We talked about past entanglements. I had once flown to Japan to see a girl who dumped me on arrival. I was there for ten days anyway, and I hit my head on everything. Amanda had a boyfriend in England still, but had snogged a male model on the flight to Prague just for fun. Our garden would be rife with marigolds, with passionflower spindling the trellis on one side, and a sundial that doubled as a birdbath.

I could not quite figure out which country or for that matter continent or hemisphere we were going to grace with our sublime abode. After we made out against a marble pillar in the music bar built by the president's grandfather, she came back to my Žižkov flat, where, for a while, there had been gold leaf on the ceiling, Art Nouveau on the walls, and beeswax on the floorboards, applied by a diligent household help in splendid livery.

EROTIC CITY

Three or four times Amanda joined us for lessons at the Golden Lion, and my students paid me no attention whatever. Ivan said she was like a south coast sunbeam, while all the other British people he knew had grown up in the same desk drawer. Vlasta shyly suggested places to shop for clothes, as if anticipating that her suggestions would be met with English derision; I think that between lessons Amanda bought a cheap black Czech cardigan just to reassure Vlasta. With Amanda present even Milan looked like a dog watching somebody juggle three tennis balls.

Ivan observed once that preserving Native American place names implied a value system distinct from that in which ancient cities were rechristened Stalingrad and Leningrad. Slavic languages and Slavic mind-sets were, he said, inherently totalitarian—whether I was Elliott, Eliottu, Elliottove, et cetera, depended on which department of a vast grammatical bureaucracy had authorized my existence in a sentence. My experience of speaking Czech was like that: Well, I need a noun. No, you must have a verb first. Okay, I'd like a verb. No, first you must furnish evidence of an object or a subject or both, without neglecting the small print affixed to these choices. But I just want a beer. You may consult your phrasebook for that, but don't imagine that you know what you're doing.

Amanda reassured him that English was just as oppressive.

Ivan and my other students were, I think, predisposed to think of things in world-historical terms partly because their destinies had been abruptly transferred from an all-powerful state to an even more powerful corporate accounting department in a clash of equally inhumane ideologies. He joked moreover that Normans slaughtering Saxons slaughtering Romans slaughtering Celts slaughtering Picts helps explain the violence that English grammar and spelling inflict on logic and common sense. He thought the capitalized first person pronoun might have given rise to the sense of smug entitlement that inspires a lust for private property, too.

Amanda wondered why Ivan needed lessons in English or anything else for that matter. I told her that he had spent some time in the States, but that he seemed very lonely to me, as in fact all my students did, and that probably he came to lessons for the ephemeral sense of companionship.

Amanda began teaching, too, but not in a pub, and I didn't get to go to her lessons. By luck or hard work or charisma or good looks or some combination thereof, she was dispatched to more demanding clients than mine: working on the top floors of investment banks and the basement offices of international law firms.

Evenings and weekends we did the standard things together: drinking to excess with other expatriate English teachers; curing our hangovers the next day with stacks of blueberry pancakes from an ostensibly American joint called Radost FX. Radost means "joy" in Czech, and they served Radegast beer, named after the ancient Slavic deity in charge of hospitality and merriment. Saturday mornings were devoted to museums and rampart views of all the Prague Castle outbuildings erected for wives by emperors and later inhabited by mistresses.

Amanda also pointed out, very early on, that there was something artificial in our arrangements in Prague. The president was a playwright who lived in a hilltop castle, and none of us had cars or children; we lived in a sort of up- or downgraded version of the set from *Friends*. She refused to buy IKEA furniture because she didn't want to live like a student anymore. Fresh teaching blood arrived once a month from New York or California and spent a few weeks inflicting a vast and suppurating wound on Daddy's credit card before going home broken and desolate. What we had profuse wealth in was time.

I was surprised and disappointed in Prague by a seeming dearth of ghost stories. I solicited them from students and asked Amanda to do the same. The headless knight of Týn church was so generic he had to be tourist fare, and the water spirit who keeps souls in jars beneath the Vltava exists only to frighten children. It seemed to me that any sufficiently spooky hole in

British or American ground necessarily has some story attached to it, even if it is just *Elvis Lives Here* scrawled in graffiti nearby. The Czechs, I thought, evinced remarkably little need to feel haunted.

Amanda's English childhood and youth always struck me as profoundly dull, as if no mere event could possibly disrupt the placid, stable, exploitative society she grew up in, or alter her own predestined trajectory. Britain was the land of eternal recurrence, where things happened the same way over and over and over again. Nothing terrible or traumatic had happened to her or her family—it was her understanding that every American had an uncle in prison. She was deeply frightened by nuns after three years at a Catholic school for girls. She had also been sent, age six, for elocution lessons with a mad Canadian woman who insisted that she throw her voice over the bridge, whatever that meant. The idea was that a regional accent might, later in life, damage her social standing or even employment prospects; the unforgivable sin in Britain was coming from somewhere.

Perhaps there were cracks in the edifice, subtle and insidious. Her grandfather had played rugby for England until his career was cut short by injury. She showed me old photos of the rugby men on seaside holidays with their families, each one clean-shaven with pressed socks up to the knee and crisply parted hair. They were all, she assured me, very drunk most of the time, yet unfailingly kind and firm with the children. Then she flipped open her laptop and showed snaps on the Bristol team's new website of men in their underwear falling off bar tables in Ibiza. Women and children were nowhere to be found. Compared to their predecessors, Amanda observed, these men's physiques were much improved by sports science.

Otherwise, I detected a childhood spent in the mud. Her

parents, inveterate ramblers, had marched her up hill and down dale from an early age, and she got her physique the honest way. It was not always raining, but never entirely dry either, and every childhood holiday story involved some combination of a creepy country pub landlord objecting to the perfect camouflage worn by all three of them. She was an only child. I had the impression that when she was not working, displaying her flawless manners and exquisite elocution, she not only hailed from Somerset; she wore it: mud, leaves, wind-blasted wool caught in her hair and all. She had never been happier than when stranded on a Bristol Channel island with a lighthouse and a monastic library where two minutes outdoors got you slathered in gull poop.

What meeting Amanda meant for me was that at last I had a walking companion. She was happy to go anywhere in any weather for the express purpose of getting lost.

During one early stroll Amanda felt a tug on her shoulder and looked up to see her handbag gaining speed in the hand of a youth riding past on a moped. There was not even a moment when anything could be done about it but listen to the moped engine revving and receding simultaneously like a can of angry bees hurled through the air. A red-and-white tram rattled through our field of vision and it was as though the handbag had never existed.

Amanda blamed herself and said, through tears, that anyone so stupid and careless deserved to be robbed; all the guidebooks warned of pickpockets. I asked what was in the handbag, and she said she had a lot of phone calls to make. Passport, driving license, credit card, to start with. I suggested making a list right away and she rallied. We dived into the nearest pub where I asked for two beers and paper and pen (miming for these as my

Czech was inadequate), and Amanda told me that her handbag itself was the real loss, a stylish and capacious maroon old soldier who had never complained.

She would need to contact her parents first to get the number for her bank in England, the British Embassy for a replacement passport, some number in Swansea for the driving license. She required a new National Insurance number card, a library card if she ever returned to live in the UK, two thousand Czech crowns meant to last until payday—fortunately she had already paid that month's rent—some new sunglasses, a new Czech phrase book, her keys, a couple of pens, an address book, and a shade of lipstick probably not available in Prague. Compiling the list cheered her up. I sensed that she was a woman of action, and I said so. She thanked me and said she was glad I was there.

Meanwhile her credit card took a thrilling illicit tour of some of Prague's sleazier districts. She was informed of this by her bank in England the following morning. It had gone to a liquor store, visited an ATM at a nightclub called Erotic City, and dined at a nearby Chinese restaurant. When I asked about the cashpoint, she said she'd told me already that she was stupid. She kept her PIN on a folded square of paper in an inside pocket of the handbag, because she had forgotten it more than once. I had a momentary vision of her as a tremendous liability to be dragged and heaved through life, forgetful and unconcerned. She totaled the car, misplaced the children, and got indicted for tax fraud while I was condemned to be the person knowledgeable about things like home insurance, plus which I never got a birthday card.

She was prompt and diligent with her phone calls and filling out forms for replacement cards; her parents undertook to cover damage to her credit card balance that the bank declined to absorb, and to send some interim cash at the earliest. The aftermath of the theft turned out to be ninety-five percent bureaucracy. And yet for the first time since landing in Prague I felt useful somehow, though I'd done nothing but lend her a few thousand crowns and make comforting sounds at appropriate intervals. Amanda continued to blame herself. Gradually it dawned on me that she had depended on me in some vital way that was unlike showing up on time or returning a library book, and that being each on our own in a strange city, in any sort of crunch we might as well be the only two people alive.

Northwest of the city—where I had walked before losing my shoes—lay a small area called Divoká Šárka, "wild wood," composed of slopes swathed in pine trees, with all the silence that implies: dramatic limestone cliffs and manic streams of snow melt; isolated quaint cottages with billowing chimneys and the reek of marijuana; and small hidden pubs to which it was unclear how supplies of beer and food were delivered. I took her there in the afternoon to distract her and clear her mind of the missing handbag.

Each of these pubs had a garden in which some item of industrial detritus had been repurposed as art. At my favorite, vast iron hinges gathered like birds on railway sleepers; we supposed they were trying to keep each other warm. Elsewhere sprockets and pulleys mustered like hostile militias; hooks and chains winked and flirted; and brackets, ferrules, spigots, and grommets formed an awkward queue inside at the bar.

"Everything here makes sense," said Amanda. "Some horrific event in living memory abides in the air and presides over subsequent proceedings. In England we only care about Eurovision."

The owner/proprietor spoke in an alien dialect so it was best to point at the beer or the menu and signal quantities with fingers. The other patrons, all men, looked as though they had preferred prison. They did not even grin when a girl of no more than ten began driving her drunken father home aboard a yellow Zetor tractor.

While we were there the president stopped by for an improbable pint between meetings with world leaders. The pub was so remote that he must have gone on purpose to escape public scrutiny, or to indulge in some sentimental simulacrum of privacy. His entourage screened him largely from view while they annihilated silence with heated consultation, and the impression we had was of governance by smoke signal—he aimed the plumes from one cigarette after another toward the ceiling, and although we could not see the man, his thoughts and instructions seemed to dissipate visibly over the heads of his inferiors. Their voices where hushed and in Czech, yet it seemed to us obvious that some sort of power struggle was occurring, with each advisor, counselor, or minister vying to sweep the field, and the president's job consisted largely in knowing when to speak. Leading a free country and managing an unruly classroom were likely one and the same thing. A similar scene in the West would have entailed handshakes and babies and cameras and sound bites, but the president's constituents ignored him respectfully.

Amanda went slowly without sudden movements to and out the door to investigate how the president traveled; when she returned she described two gleaming porpoiselike Mercedes sedans flanked by scowling men the size and shape of refrigerators. The cars were up for any frolic but their handlers weren't. I had the same sense of the invisible president: he would have envied us exploring his beautiful homeland whimsically without destination, but his thankless task was to run it.

What followed was inexplicable at the time and surreal on reflection. A door adjacent to the bar opened and four partially attired young ladies emerged—this at four in the afternoon. The president's men formed a human shield instantaneously—as though any one of the ladies might possess a lethal weapon, though no obvious place to conceal it. The ladies, all smiles and eyelashes, made for tables of grumpy men, who paid them no more attention than they had to the president or anyone else. We were not approached. The president's men implored him urgently to action. I hallucinated the sound of spurs on a boardwalk and wondered why there was no piano player. The president, judging from the roiling cloud overhead, had decided to finish his cigarette. The girls, rebuffed, looked lost and hurt, unsure where to turn. The president's men formed a gauntlet to the door and propelled him—the president of love and truth—to the safety of his car.

A man emerged from the door by the bar, around his neck the sort of camera that could distinguish the eyelash hairs of a honeybee. We could see that the course of history had nearly swerved. He tried to explain to the girls in polite British English that they would not be paid after all. They refused to be soothed. Amanda was despondent afterward, as if something she had fled had pursued her to the most nondescript, nonsensical, and innocent place on any map.

PIGEON 1 (A)

I lived, when I was seven, for a year in Lincolnshire, which is very flat and much like Indiana, with cabbage instead of corn. It was a perfect place to invade; just roll your tank off the boat and ask for directions. There was an RAF base nearby and pillboxes everywhere filled with moldering pornography and wholesome graffiti like KILROY WOZ ERE—very civilized vandalism by later standards. Dad taught in a huge manor house that functioned as the overseas campus of his university. Mom was invited to lots of different houses for afternoon tea. My brother went to Isaac Newton's old school in Grantham, and on his first day the other boys threw him in the River Witham with his school uniform on. My sister went to Margaret Thatcher's alma mater, where the other girls made her cry every day for sport. My school was walking distance from our cottage. On my first day, the other kids said, "Hey American, we could have won the war without you." I didn't know what they were talking about. There were Harrier jets prepping for the Falklands overhead, and I would have preferred talking about those, because I thought Harrier Jump Jets were pretty fucking cool.

I probably fell in love with Amanda fifteen years before we met, when a girl of my age named Sophie stuck her tongue out at me while I queued with my family to receive Communion at the church of St. Wulfram, whichever degenerate and parochial bastard he was, in Grantham. Sophie wore a pale blue choir frock and her sandy blond hair in a ponytail. She was angelic and rude like Amanda.

The door to the apartment stood at the top of two flights of wide marble stairs in an Art Nouveau building in the Jewish Quarter, the façade adorned with stylized pharaohs and brickwork meant to resemble mother-of-pearl. The Spanish Synagogue was across the street. All the best bars and newest restaurants were five minutes' walk away.

As he showed us into the flat, the estate agent was evasive. The date of the building was unknown, the cost of utilities uncertain, the previous tenants untalkative, but probably Russian. The landlady he'd met only once was certainly Russian, or at least no Czech woman was ever named Maja. Some of the furnishings—decorative plates on gold-plated stands atop an unpainted plywood bookshelf—might have been Ukrainian folk art, but he didn't know if that stuff would remain. It didn't. The number of tenants with access to our own future stairwell if we signed the lease was somewhere between twelve and sixteen, but the building itself was a quadrangular complex with access to each façade and an indeterminate number of communal and maintenance doorways. There was, somewhere, an elevator, or possibly more than one. He was unsure how long the flat had been on the market.

Amanda asked the questions, though none of the answers mattered. She was tired of my elbows and knees when we slept on my pullout sofa in Žižkov, and we were both exhausted by the carnival of trolls, ogres, and deviants at Hotel Doom. We had known each other only two months, but met daily and shared all, and we were determined to start and end each day with conversations over the same pillow. We could argue, of course, later over the size and color of the pillow, or get several. First we needed a roof.

And perversely, we loved the flat. Some previous tenant had painted the bedroom walls a lurid brothel pink; instead of repainting it Amanda bought faux leopard skin rugs and a zebra stripe duvet. We called the place Graceland. The kitchen floor had a fever of black-and-white tiles in fragments glued back together, and one sky-blue wall with framed pictures of esoteric plants captioned in Latin. Opposite the blue wall stood a substantial piece of cabinetry installed sometime in the last days of the Austro-Hungarian Empire. The vertical surfaces of this cabinetry were all stained and gashed with mysterious evidence of events in the distant past, as if a previous tenant had a penchant for throwing cats. Our bathtub was sufficient for two people to sit in with books, hot drinks, and ashtrays in the evenings. We had a running dispute about whether Matisse or Mucha should preside over the bedroom; I favored Mucha because of his local origin and affiliations, but Amanda thought him too commercial and suspected that I just wanted a lovely nymphet to look at every morning. Without telling me, she bought and had framed the kind of Matisse print in which six blobs of paint implied a humanoid figure, but it did look very good on the wall, and she invited me to choose something for the bathroom.

The only drawback to the place was a German toilet with a shelf of the lay-and-display kind. You deposited your product on a kind of dry shelf where you could inspect it for clues to your health before flushing. Toilet fashion had since evolved in Germany, we gathered, but we were stuck with a relic of another era.

We had been there only two weeks when a neighbor fell to his death from a fourth-floor balcony facing a courtyard. We didn't witness the event or see the body. Amanda answered a knock on the door one Saturday morning and found a police officer who spoke no English on the other side. After some initial confusion the officer recruited our neighbor Gabi to translate. Gabi did not speak English either, but she and Amanda spoke the same stripe of French.

The man, in his seventies, had been feeding pigeons. Had we known him? Seen anything? I went to our balcony to look.

In summer weather through open windows we heard invisible fathers yelling at invisible mothers who yelled at invisible children who cried. "Bohemians are not very bohemian," said Amanda. We avoided the balcony and the courtyard because it gave us the feeling of having passed from the first world thrum of street level into some dire pocket of deepest Ukraine; we had in our flat some comfort and security, but just over the balcony's edge lay ravaging want and madness.

The courtyard was a shadowy box canyon full of rear windows, laundry lines, and garbage. The three police officers below were the first people I had seen in it. One officer offered a cigarette to another. The third was peering up. I thought I dimly remembered a diminutive white-haired man so wiry he might have just slipped through the balcony's iron grate.

When the officer had gone Amanda and I both felt a need to get out of the flat. We walked forty-five minutes to the nearest croissant at the French Institute café, and we shared the *International Herald Tribune* over coffee. We didn't discuss the dead man. By unspoken agreement that could wait. Suddenly it seemed that our courtyard might be haunted.

We wandered over the river to an unfamiliar area. Both of us happily agreed that the purpose of a long walk is to get lost. Mission accomplished, we washed sandwiches down with beer in an unfamiliar bar and somehow made our way slowly home, where we found a police summons taped to our door with a handwritten explanation in French by Gabi. If we were unable to find a willing translator one would be provided for us.

PIGEON 2 (B)

The uses of communist-era buildings remained controversial, particularly those in which people were tortured and killed. The police station, Ivan explained to us as he drove us there, occupied a structure where nothing terrible was known to have happened, yet the archives of who informed on whom had been kept there. Everyone agreed it would have been better to locate the police force in a temple of violence than a shrine to mistrust, but the authorities imagined that they were being sensitive. We pulled up to a long domino of a plate glass and granite building, and Ivan led the way inside and announced us at the reception desk.

We were called in for questioning and were about to experience a feeling that Czechs of Ivan's generation must have had every day. There was a permanent dread in the air. The detec-

tive was in his fifties, judging from the proportion of grey to
white in his hair and mustache and the lines engraved in his
jowls. Before he had put one question to us through Ivan I had
formulated several: Had he held his job through the revolution? If so, what had his role been in the suppression of dissent
before and during it? Under what conditions had he begun his
job, and how had he advanced without being purged when
the wind changed? Why wasn't he working part-time in a factory or drinking beer and feeling ostracized in his home village? There was a Czech saying Ivan had told me about that
under communism it was okay to be ahead of your time, but
not by more than about six months. The political sensibilities
of those who weathered the transition were suspect. Elsewhere
senior bankers were converting state assets into Spanish and
Portuguese villas for their families through suspect privatiza-
tion schemes, seasoned politicians were consolidating power
in association with known villains, and entire towns were
being turned over to Russian mafiosi, along with much of the
national infrastructure—our policeman was likely quite tame
as rogues go. When Czech people hear British and American
people grumbling about shady politicians, said Amanda, later,
they must want to pat us on the head.

Fortunately we had Ivan, like Virgil, as our guide. The detec-
tive and Ivan exchanged flurries of Czech, and Ivan turned to
us and said, "Inspector Sokol apologizes for the inconvenience,
but says that sadly he cannot question the pigeons."

Both men spoke for a while as if Amanda and I were not
there, with Ivan pausing occasionally to summarize what had
been said. The inspector wanted to know our jobs, legal status,
length of stay to date and intended length of stay if known, and
how we came to be the sole foreigners in our building. Ivan

was able to answer all of the above on our behalf. While they talked I examined the room, trying to figure out which division we were in: there was no helpful sign reading *Homicide* or *Larceny* in English. Various notices in Czech were pinned to a pegboard, and an electric typewriter sat next to a rotary phone on the inspector's desk, but it was not his office—it was too clean for that. It was a space for taking statements. I had not noticed initially that we were being recorded.

The inspector asked whether we had ever observed or spoken to our unfortunate neighbor. Neither of us could remember doing so. Had we noticed, observed, or heard anything on the afternoon or evening in question? We had not. Amanda remained calm and cool throughout; I kept expecting the inspector to break into English and say, *This will go down on your permanent record,* or for us to be dragged to a small cell.

He continued: How well did we know our other neighbors? Not at all, except for the owner of the beagle who greeted all passersby on the second-floor landing whenever she was cleaning.

The inspector leaned back in his chair and considered the ceiling before speaking to Ivan at length in carefully chosen words; Ivan leaned back in his chair and considered the ceiling before delivering a carefully worded translation; the manner in which we received the information was of the nature of a mouse traveling through a snake.

"There is little or nothing suspicious," said Ivan, "says the inspector. But the man in question was a known wanker."

I looked at Amanda in hopes she would know whether this was meant literally or figuratively.

"In the sense of a public nuisance, or an unpleasant person?" I said.

"A tosser? A twat?" said Amanda. Ivan plunged into his dictionary.

"A dickhead?" I said.

"An asshole," said the inspector, in English.

"An informant," said Ivan, not looking up.

TRIUMPH

We never learned the man's name nor how many lives he had ruined or in what ways. Apparently you could just say, under communism, *Elliott belongs to the jazz club,* and thus sentence Elliott to ten years in prison, and the point, as far as I could tell, was not that Elliott was a dangerous radical but that in prison there is no jazz. In other respects communism sounded pretty grand to me. I had several students who were nostalgic for the days when your only obligation was beer in the garden on a summer afternoon because there wasn't any work to do but there was total job security. Under the new Western rules there still wasn't any work to do but you had to look busy. The notion that work itself was somehow virtuous had been foolishly imported.

Some of the dead man's things appeared on a wooden bookshelf, presumably his, inside the foyer of our building, with a sign in Czech declaring all of it free. There were some egg cups, a couple of framed nudes in pencil, several books in Czech and two in Russian, a blue vase of famed Bohemian crystal, some lamps, a clock, an apron, several worn and distinguished men's caps, a Florida postcard with *Wish You Were Here* in English on one side and Czech scribble on the other (did the man have a child or children studying, vacationing, or living in America?), a mirror, some plants, various spices, a transistor radio, a miniature glazed Buddha, a one-piece woman's swimsuit with fraying elastic around the edges, some swimming goggles, and a stack of newspapers.

"We could use that mirror for the hallway," I suggested.

"I don't want to look in it every day and wonder if I'm a wanker, too," said Amanda.

She pulled out the newspapers—all of them yellowing and dating from the late '70s—and said she hoped they captured some pivotal moment in the man's life so that we could at least learn his name. Although we couldn't read the papers we soon discovered that their common denominator was not him but an Olympic swimmer—a beautiful Czech woman photographed at moments of triumph, receiving medals, plaques, and accolades, giving interviews. She had a different smile for each photographer but never appeared without one, and she always met the camera with bright inquisitive eyes. The swimsuit in one newspaper photo appeared to be the same as the swimsuit next to the glazed Buddha. The only thing we gleaned about our deceased neighbor was that he had once been in love.

Neither of us slept well for the following week. I dreamed in agitation of pigeons and swimmers, and I dreamed of conversation and intimacies on the balcony with Amanda, shattered by one or the other or both of us falling fifty feet. One morning I was inspired to suggest marriage and she burst into laughter. The idea had come to me in a paroxysm of fear; anything could happen to anybody at any time, and the only defense was to agree that it wasn't going to happen between us.

"I am not here," said Amanda, "to be your last resort."

One of our neighbors at Graceland was a German woman named Sonja with a nuance-smashing communication style. Amanda said that she felt the purpose of any question Sonja asked was really to say, *What's wrong with you?* Sonja told me privately that as an American I was at least capable of direct speech, unlike, presumably, the decorous Czechs and the wily British. She was from Düsseldorf, but she worked for the EU. She had been successively posted to Brussels, Strasbourg, and Prague, which sounded like a career going downhill but represented growing autonomy and responsibility. It also involved a sickening deterioration in the standards of public swimming pools and teeth, among other things. She returned to Germany as often as possible, where she swam twice a day and got her teeth polished often.

I found her rifling through the dead man's things in the foyer one evening when I got home from work. She was looking through the newspaper clippings in particular, and it turned out that her interest in swimming paid off. The woman pictured, she told me, had broken a toe poolside at the 1968 Summer Olympics in Mexico City, but swam anyway to claim the silver in the women's 200-meter freestyle, losing to her East German adversary by one-tenth of a second—a difference surely attributable to the toe and the distraction the pain shooting through her leg must have caused her. When asked later by an international press gang how she had broken her toe, she said, "Oh, I can't do anything right on land." After that she was applauded and admired much more than the gold medalist, who sulked over losing the limelight.

The newspaper didn't say, but Sonja knew, that later that month the swimmer defected, and never returned to Prague.

The Soviet tanks rolled into the Old Town Square in August, said Sonja, and the Olympics were held in October, and in November in Vienna the United Nations ratified the most successful international treaty of all time, the Convention on Road Signs and Signals. I began to worry that what lay ahead was some kind of German conversation in which everything is equally interesting. Sonja's father had worked for the West German ministry of the environment, and he had told Sonja dozens of stories of Czechs and Slovaks escaping the Soviet occupation on skis and canoes into Austria. Negotiations over stop signs and speed limits took place in an atmosphere of dread and dismay, and Vienna's Red Cross shelters were full of Czechoslovak refugees. The year 1968 was also the beginning of the Open Era in tennis, when professionals were invited to compete against amateurs. I already knew that since Milan had mentioned it many times, and could seemingly supply the names of champions of every major tournament for any given year since.

The Olympic swimmer's defection had been on everyone's lips in Vienna. She had said she was taking a short walk to test her toe. Of course she was being followed, but the Mercedes waiting for her was unexpected. Afterward it was thought that she had broken her toe on purpose, or perhaps that she had not broken it at all. A further mystery was how such a person could be of any value or consequence to the West; that is, who sent the car and why.

Sonja did not know where the swimmer had defected to

and suggested that perhaps she had been given a new identity. "But," I said, "she was briefly in every newspaper in the world. Surely she would be noticed."

"You think people are that observant?" said Sonja, and it did sound like *What's wrong with you?*

Her views raised a whole suite of questions about our newly deceased neighbor. Had the swimmer obtained valuable intelligence from him? Had he turned nasty after or because of her defection? What if, after the revolution, they had made contact, and she wrote that she was happy in Des Moines, that her three children had simple strong American names and spoke only English? I asked Sonja if she had ever spoken to the man.

"Twice," she said. "Once he helped me at the front door with some groceries. He said I should shop at the *potraviny* instead of the *lahůdky* because better selection and lower prices. It felt like a criticism, but he was right."

"Did he tell you his name?"

"If so, I have forgotten. The other occasion was a sunny day when he suggested I should grab a man and go boating. I thought that somewhat rude, too. As though he pitied my solitary condition."

"Well, did you?"

"No. The river is filthy."

I asked if she knew anything else about him, whether she had ever seen him on the street or run into him at the *lahůdky* or the *potraviny.* For that matter as a Czech man he must have had a nearby barstool accustomed to his presence.

"Yes," she said, "but the Czechs keep strange hours. The elderly all ride the Metro at rush hour, have you noticed? So they can be reassured they aren't dead yet."

I thought of my Žižkov landlady and how I never saw or

heard her go out. Those vile pastries had to originate somewhere. I noticed after speaking to Sonja that on the Metro every
young woman was beautiful and every young man was injured.
Canes and crutches and casts, eye patches, bandages, and back
braces; I put it down to the national love of ice hockey, tennis, and skiing. Yet she was right about rush hour, too. Whenever you needed to get somewhere you had to elbow hordes of
stooped grey-haired women and bald crippled old men, and
none of them had any companion or compelling reason for
rushing across town at 7:30 a.m., unless they were all seeing the
same doctor, simultaneously. I thought this must be what happens if you never learn trust. Fortunately the communists were
extremely good at public transport and all the stations were
very attractive. Each tunnel was lined with space-age aluminum panels in thoughtful color schemes, featuring either large
bubbles or indentations, convex and concave, breasts and anti-
breasts, all the length of the platform. My favorite station was
Pankrác, because it sounded like "punk rock," until Vlasta told
me it was the site of a famous prison where more than a thousand people were guillotined during the Second World War.

DES MOINES

Miloš Forman, Milan Kundera, and Martina Navratilova all struck me as a wonderful roster of late-twentieth-century Czech achievement, and a beautiful contrast to the previous seven centuries of Bohemian bloodshed. Directing *Amadeus,* writing *The Unbearable Lightness of Being,* and triumphing nine times at Wimbledon were all laudable aims and achievements. The question I had—planted in my head by my students—was why those three had all chosen to live somewhere else, as though Prague weren't good enough.

America was, of course, apparently not good enough for me. It contained guns and Republicans and megachurches and personal injury lawyers and five square meters of television screen per household, headache-inducing beer, and far, far too much space that was relentlessly paved. It had laws determined by pressure groups, a language debased by idiots, and a mythology based on subliterate kids chasing cattle.

"Are there," said Milan, "many Indians in Indiana?"

"There aren't many anythings in Indiana," I said. "Particularly Indians."

"You left to escape the loneliness," suggested Milan.

"I hadn't thought of it as escaping until I got here," I said.

I thought to myself later that in addition to the surplus space in America, there was always and also too much time. An hour in Indiana could last all day, the sun at a standstill and the mostly rotund residents shuffling toward air-conditioned cars they drove slowly past corn in the fields that was too sleepy to watch itself grow. There was also all the time necessary to cross all that space; an hour or two in the car every day. A job under American conditions would be intolerable, no task ever quite finished yet not enough to do. Daytime TV just elongated the hours further.

"We listen," said Milan, "to a lot of American music."

Vlasta was there but Ivan was away investigating the marriage of a forklift and somebody's sternum. "I am interested," she said, "in rappers who show respect to their mothers."

"They exist," I said.

" 'Mama Said Knock You Out,' " said Milan.

"That's a very high bar," I said.

"*Crib*—this means 'bed,' yes?—for my mom on the outskirts of Philly," said Vlasta.

"I think that has more to do with the man's earning potential," I said.

"Yes, but he bought his mother a bed."

"A house," I said.

"Okay," said Milan. "A little shout-out to my dad and mom."

"You may know this stuff better than I do," I said.

"What I hear," said Vlasta, "is mainly concerned with bitches and hos."

"Also much motherfucking. The gentlemen stand out," said Milan.

"Perhaps they do," I said. "Do either of you have children?"

"None that I know of," said Milan.

"I have two," said Vlasta. "One boy and one girl ages fifteen and twelve. Kuba is my oldest. Short for Jakub. He gets in trouble at school but I am very proud of him. Recently he made the Hitler salute to his class and said this is how high my dog jumps when I come home."

"You have a dog?"

"No. Hanka takes after her father. He is in Switzerland with a sophisticated Western woman. They are wealthy and yet sometimes I must pay the train fares for the children to see him."

"Do you go with them?" said Milan.

"No. Kuba is old enough to look after his sister."

"Yes," said Milan, "but you could drop them off and treat yourself to some skiing."

"It would not be enjoyable," said Vlasta.

"Elliott," said Milan, "I think you must teach Vlasta sophistication."

"Sure," I said. "First lesson is how to order a Happy Meal."

"Sometimes," said Vlasta, "the way the children speak to me is awful. Like their father. *Shut up. Go away. Leave me alone.* Always it is worse when they return. They become agents of the devil, serving up little slices of hell. I worry that they will inherit their father's inability to perceive the suffering of others."

"Perhaps Elliott can teach you how to swear at them," said Milan.

"Perhaps you could just buy them Angry Meals," I said.

"You're going to be rich, Elliott," said Milan.

"It gets worse as they get older," said Vlasta. "They prefer some things there. They prefer everything that costs more, basically. When I am walking Hanka to school and holding her hand and she is dragging her heels I feel that what I am really doing is dragging her father. Even though he has two good adult legs."

"The only defense against capitalism is nostalgia," said Milan. "That makes children especially vulnerable."

"The only defense for a parent is love," said Vlasta. "And it doesn't work."

Milan said that he had detected an epidemic of women who had men who were dreadful liabilities, whether chronically underemployed, or blackout drunk every night, or prone to frightening the children. He wouldn't mind companionship, he said, but becoming or taking on liabilities, well, he was risk-averse.

"Do you always talk about love like an insurance product?" said Vlasta.

"There is nothing inherently wrong with insurance," he said.

"It's based entirely on fear," I said.

"Fear is a perfectly valid biological fight-or-flight motivator," he said. "If you suppress it you can focus on other things."

"Like what?" I said. "The TV?"

"You could at least have a companion to watch it with," said Vlasta.

"Inspiring," said Milan. "I'll start searching tomorrow."

Listening to them bicker, I was reminded how much older

they were: constrained by past choices, navigating ever-narrower channels toward largely foregone conclusions. The idea that you might meet somebody beneath the astronomical clock and together outrun the sun was preposterous.

Elsewhere, capitalism metastasized. First there were Whirlpool and Nike logos on the sides of trams. Then the advertisements on the Metro—even if your Czech reading abilities were rudimentary—began to promise exclusive honey from pedigreed bees, organic milk from intellectual cows, sound educations for deserving children, and you could even learn German in three weeks. Sports facilities throughout the city were renamed after multinational corporations. The buildings that retained their old names seemed quaint, like the National Theatre, suggesting there once was a nation that aspired to have a theater, although you could equally argue that the august concert hall called the Rudolfinum was named after the emperor Rudolf II before multinational conglomerates elbowed emperors out of the way.

There was a nightly TV weather forecast watched and beloved by all or most or perhaps only half of the Czech nation. It consisted of a beautiful woman rising naked from bed and dressing appropriately for the following morning, a striptease in reverse. What began with titillation quickly gave way to worry about whether she was going to be warm enough in what she was wearing. The show aired at midnight, and each viewer was sent to sleep with mild anxiety about the day ahead. It was common after watching an erotic-meteorological performance to have nightmares about catastrophic weather events.

The more I thought about the balcony man, the more convinced I became of his terrible isolation and profound self-loathing, this pariah whose only experience of conviviality was a confederation of squabbling pigeons who did not judge him. Whatever human relationships he had ever had compromised, and whatever vitality he had ever possessed spent. I began to picture him in my daydreams and in my sleep, playing tennis. I could not fix his face in my mind, old or young, but I could feel the exhilaration of a good serve and the humiliation of a weak return, even though I only ever tried playing once myself. I could hear the ball meeting the racket and feel the need to wipe sweat from my forehead before it reached my eyes. Or I pictured him in the water with his swimmer, hopelessly outclassed and charmed, trying to come up with invitations that weren't too obvious. I tried to imagine a life of which the central event was someone else's broken toe. Which toe was it? The newspapers wouldn't necessarily record a detail like that. The archives detailing whom he had got sent to the uranium mines and why would be altogether devoid of interest. Did his swimmer cook for him, or he for her, and if so, what?

I pictured him, frail and elderly, walking into a library or a bookshop intent on learning every possible thing about Des Moines. That is, I imagined him imagining her life, desperate to know where she bought her groceries, terrified that in that and other respects Des Moines might not be a suitable place. Perhaps he checked a map, saw numbered streets on an alien grid, hostile to comprehension. I imagined his vexation at not being able to check the Iowa forecast every day. Above all I felt unbearably sad that whoever and wherever she was, she had no way of knowing what had happened to him.

"I would imagine," said Amanda, "that she has moved on." We were in the bathtub again, but on a Saturday morning with coffee and books and a small selection of cold meats from the *lahudky.* "If they were ever involved. Why are you so sure he wasn't simply investigating her disappearance?"

"I guess I don't think wankers investigated things," I said. "They left that up to the cocksuckers."

"I expect she was a target," said Amanda. "Or that he was just a perv."

"He didn't have a file on her," I said. "Just the photos and clippings of an admirer."

"Or a creep."

"Those are synonyms," I said.

"People see what they want to see," said Amanda.

"Maybe," I said, "he helped her escape."

Amanda had already returned to her book. I was only twenty-four, and I hadn't hurt anybody yet.

PART II

BROTHERS

Time passed in spurts that pooled here and splashed there. Coin colonies took over Graceland, piles of crowns and hellers I discharged from my pockets when I got home, which irritated Amanda immensely. Coffee, bagels, and burgers improved throughout the city center, but prices didn't. The poor hellers like surplus labor took shelter with me.

One morning alone together over beer in the Golden Lion, Milan told me that he had had a twin brother named Ludvik. When the boys were about a year old their mother was bathing them before bedtime, but she went to chat with a neighbor, and when she returned an hour later one of the twins had drowned.

It was easy and reasonable to pin the blame on their father. He had a couple of witnesses who were reasonably sure he had been in the pub at the time, but she had numerous witnesses to testify that he drank three liters of brandy every day. It was her word against his and she won. Off went the father to prison, although negligence and manslaughter were apparently not serious crimes, and he was back at his pub a year later. Meanwhile the judgment and behavior of the mother went before the court of neighborly opinion.

She was a scatterbrained chatterbox to begin with, or the tragedy would never have occurred. Afterward, said Milan, her judgment and behavior became increasingly erratic, although he was too young to know it then. Only she had ever been able to tell the children apart, and at first it was widely accepted that Ludvik, not Milan, had drowned. But increasingly she called Milan Ludvik, so that in his first memories he was a child named Ludvik whose brother Milan had drowned. There was no real reason why he couldn't or shouldn't go through life under the one name instead of the other, but only his mother called him Ludvik, so when he started school he became Ludvik at home and Milan in the world. The divergence between home life and school life did not stop there. At home he fed himself—exclusively sweets—and went to sleep by collapsing at midnight while his mother babbled or sobbed or passed out on the sofa from all the rum in her hot chocolate. She was never emotionally distant, he said, but she knew how to cling and not how to protect, and through maternal channels difficult to analyze she passed all her grief and guilt straight to him.

Who he was mattered to him increasingly. Other children announced or displayed an allegiance or preference for one parent or another, but Milan couldn't even get that far. He determined early on that he had little in common with either parent, but he didn't even know who he was. He did not enjoy school, but found it less unbearable than life at home. Girls avoided him, and boys tormented him, which meant that fortunately he never confessed his secret to some merciless small person of his own age.

Milan was a teenager before it occurred to him that perhaps he had actively murdered his brother. At the least it seemed likely that they had played some baby game together in which Milan had not understood the consequences of his actions. His waking and sleeping hours were filled with images of him sitting on his brother's head. More important, he did not know as a teenager whether he was Milan or Ludvik, and it seemed to matter, and he didn't trust his mother's account. He began to believe that either Milan or Ludvik was still alive, and that the whole drowning story was cooked up to cover some other nefarious thing. He couldn't leave home without looking for the other boy, often seeming to catch sight of him on a passing tram or cycling the other way over cobblestones with his teeth rattling. He also couldn't stay home, because he had grown to loathe his mother. His father had long ago become a kind of prostitute, living with any woman who consented to keep him in drink.

He insisted on seeing his brother's grave, but his mother refused to take him or tell him where it was. Enraged, he knocked her down. Not, he said, because of her refusal, but because he discovered that the grave had gone unvisited for years.

The means of self-destruction available to a young man in communist Czechoslovakia were severely limited. There were no hard drugs to do or violent gangs to join. There were endless ways to get in trouble with the law, but none of them very therapeutic. He covered his bedroom walls in pictures of beautiful lakes until one day, realizing what he had subconsciously done, he burned all of them. He experimented with various kinds of self-harm but concluded that he was squeamish and cowardly. He began playing tennis so that he could pretend that his opponent was his long-lost brother, Milan. A volley returned signified some human presence on the other side of the net, defying the human absence Milan keenly felt in every other arena of his life.

Once a month since before Milan could remember, his father's brother had paid a visit. As a rule he stayed exactly ten minutes, paid no attention to the child, and spoke to his sister-in-law scornfully, impatiently, like, said Milan, a doctor confronted by an epidemic and a silly woman at the same time. Milan's uncle did something within a succession of government ministries. Milan never knew what, but it was evident from the uncle's villa in Krč that his best friends lived in Moscow. Communication between Milan's mother and father occurred exclusively through Uncle Jiří, whose opinion of his own brother lay somewhere south of his opinion of his sister-in-law.

Milan was fairly sure that Uncle Jiří worked on very sensitive matters. The tunnel he burned through his brain with a Browning after the revolution suggested he had something to hide. As an adult Milan surmised that Uncle Jiří probably worked for the KGB, not the Czech security services, thus making him a traitor to his own people twice over. Yet adult Milan also surmised that Uncle Jiří's regular visits had nothing to do with his mother's well-being and everything to do with his.

He never forgot Milan's birthday. It was the only visit in a given year when Uncle Jiří spoke to him directly until he turned fifteen. On that occasion Uncle Jiří gave him a pair of Nikes, forever after a mystery of provenance and purpose. Then he brutally announced to Milan's mother that he was taking the child camping for a week. Milan had no interest in camping, particularly not with Uncle Jiří, but questioning orders was not a viable option, and Jiří told him to pack before he tried the shoes on.

Uncle Jiří had no children of his own, no affection for or interest in them, and adult Milan guessed that Uncle Jiří had about five minutes per week for women. They walked briskly to the train station in silence, Milan sensing that there was nothing recreational about the expedition; that Uncle Jiří needed Milan in order to perform some sort of job. They did not speak on the train or at the far station, six miles from Prague. When they arrived at Uncle Jiří's country cottage—a two-room wooden cabin about a mile and a quarter from the station and unsuitable for year-round habitation—Uncle Jiří told Milan to lay a fire in the woodstove. Milan felt he was being tested. Jiří then opened a trap door in the floor and from it produced two bottles of beer. They drank in silence until Jiří handed Milan a package of sausages and a block of cheese and told him to make dinner. When they had eaten they drank in silence again. There were several books in the cabin including a whole shelf of samizdat material, covertly photocopied or furtively printed, without cover art or any appeal to a reader beyond the words themselves, that Milan dared not ask about. Uncle Jiří noticed him looking and said that although that material was prohibited, keeping abreast of it was part of his job, and Milan was unlikely to come to any harm reading some of it if he wished. Uncle Jiří unfolded a cot and poured them each a slivovice before taking the bedroom for himself. Milan might have enjoyed being drunk had he not been so terrified of his uncle. He went to sleep with his new shoes on.

In the morning after Milan had brewed coffee and made

breakfast, Uncle Jiří beckoned him outside. He reached into a wooden chest on the front porch and came up with a large, well-used, but well-cared-for ax.

Milan told me that, whatever the truth, he preferred to remember his uncle as a gruff woodcutter, and that he thought Uncle Jiří probably preferred to see himself in this light, too.

"Your mother," said Uncle Jiří, bouncing the haft on his palm, "is a lunatic. I should have drowned your father when I had a chance. Your name is Milan."

Just outside the cabin stood the remains of an apple orchard—a dozen neglected trees, evenly spaced. Jiří led Milan to the nearest tree and handed the ax to him.

"This," he said, pointing at the tree, "is not your brother. It's not your mother or your father or your grumpy uncle Jiří, either. It's a fucking tree. Now kill it."

Milan had never tackled a tree before, but Jiří was patient and helpful. "Let your long arms do the work," he said. "It's more technique than muscle. Aim is more important than strength. Take your time." Halfway through the first tree Milan had developed a respectable stroke.

"I think you can do two trees a day," said Jiří. "This includes chopping them into firewood. I will show you how to use the wedge. I will be in the cabin or on the porch. I want to hear you shout your name with every stroke."

For the next six days Milan felled trees while shouting his name, and he felt that he had experienced some method of extracting confessions perfected by the KGB. They rarely spoke except when Uncle Jiří gave orders. Milan thought that instead of shouting his own name he should be shouting the names of his neighbors, or instead of maiming trees he should be maiming humans to prove his commitment to the cause or, perhaps, to simplify things, he should be attacking his neighbors while denouncing them. At one point Milan shouted his name and an elderly man walking past on the road stopped and turned to say, "Yes?"

But at the end of the week, Milan was emphatically Milan. Uncle Jiří gave him the keys to the cottage and told him to use it as he pleased. At first Milan made only tentative overnight visits, afraid that Uncle Jiří would appear. By the time he turned sixteen, he had essentially moved in. Winter was harsh, but he was creative, and initially well stocked with firewood—if you bang two pieces together and they thud, they're not ready. When they knock, you can burn them. Train delays could mean missing school. Uncle Jiří did check in now and then, and told him never to have guests except women, and even then to hide the prohibited books. He never again intervened.

One morning when he was seventeen Milan took his father a bottle of brandy but demanded to see his brother's grave before handing it over. With such an inducement, his father had little choice. The headstone, said Milan, was a simple granite slab with LUDVIK JEZDEC engraved and painted with fresh gold leaf.

ALLEGRO, LARGHETTO

During a grey wet miserable weekend Amanda spotted a chastity belt in a shop window and suggested we go to an exhibition of torture devices. I had some trouble following her logic. She had stopped explaining things and simply expected compliance instead. She was tired of the cinema and I was tired of art galleries and both of us had found the afternoon recitals of Charles University graduate music students disappointing. That left us with more clothes shopping at the British chain stores colonizing the city center and turning it into a slick and soulless High Street. We had acquired since moving into Graceland six months previously a comfortable futon, some optimal reading cushions, and filled most of a shelf with good books from the English-language bookshop. It should have been an ideal redoubt for lazy weekends. Yet something in the city or the building or the courtyard itself emanated misery. Sorrowful stories like airborne diseases made their way through the windows and under the doorframe, bubbled up through the bathtub drain. It was possible to fill Graceland with light and color and music and the smell of good food, and yet the flat was like a patient with some untreatable condition, and we got tired of palliative care.

The exhibition was in a cylindrical cannon tower called Daliborka on the eastern flank of Prague Castle. The legend of the tower was disputed—its original prisoner was named Dalibor, and one account held that he passed the time awaiting his execution by playing the violin, and all the medieval townsfolk were treated daily to sweet melancholy music. The other account held that the "violin" was a medieval torture device.

Rain in Prague dispenses double meanings; other places sport reflections but every spire in a puddle in Prague or headlight diffused on wet pavement suggests some place equally beautiful where things work correctly, probably in Bavaria. When a car in the rain leaves pavement for cobblestone the light it casts stages its own silent revolution, and the shadows scurry like rats.

Admission was a hundred Czech crowns each. I had casually remarked a week earlier to Amanda that what stuff costs was my least favorite genre of conversation, and she had needled me with it five or six times daily ever since, usually by pointing out how many beers I could buy with any amount in question. I surrendered eight beers for the two of us and we filed in.

Glass cases on trestle tables ringed a circular hall of stone floors, walls, and ceiling. In the center was an oubliette beneath an ancient, heavy iron grate, but it was unlit below, so there was no indication of how deep or cramped it was. Inside the glass cases were various contraptions with placards explaining them.

Some were straightforward: the "Ear Chopper" was a metal helmet with pivoting razor blades probably used more as a threat than a mutilator. It might have been helpful to a hairdresser who specialized in children. Several of the worst items were blamed on the Spanish—Spanish boots for crippling, a Spanish tickler for flaying, a Spanish spider for lifting victims into the air by the buttocks, belly, or breasts, or in some cases the eyes and ears. Most innocent in appearance yet perhaps most heinous was the Pear of Anguish, a pretty metal bulb, pear-like closed but umbrella-like open, which could be placed into any orifice deemed sinful (including the mouth, for heretics) and slowly expanded.

"I fancy a fruit salad," said Amanda.

A stone staircase led to an upper floor devoted to eight empty doorless prison cells; I thought it could make a good office plan with a meeting room upstairs. As we ascended to the upper floors the cells got roomier and fewer, and the top floor, for landowning political prisoners, was a single room with views through the machicolations over the city. It was lunacy not renting it out for ten thousand beers a month. In a glass case on a spindly table lay a violin clearly manufactured by Yamaha sometime within the past twenty years. A placard referred to Smetana's opera about Dalibor and suggested that this colorful legend clearly captured the true spirit of the Czech people.

Amanda suggested finding a concert somewhere, and I reminded her that the *Don Giovanni* we had seen might as well have been mounted by toddlers. There was music in Prague but much of it seemed commensurate with the sophistication of its captive tourist audience. You would need local advice to find the good stuff. Amanda accused me of cynicism.

She found the fluffiest of Mozart recitals in the listings of a free expat magazine. Outside, the clouds were in tatters and the sidewalks steaming, the city refreshed, and the gilded spires gleamed. We walked down a cobbled hillside road lined with embassies, through a tranche of sidewalk cafés like a field hospital for exhausted pedestrians, where all the waiters were wiping tables and chairs dry with tea towels, and into a small unremarkable chapel where the Stadler Quintet, among other things, was to be played.

From the first note it seemed to me that the clarinetist was extracting a confession from his instrument while the string players gently sawed at their stylized representations of human bodies, each with an expression as if to say, *This won't hurt a bit.* Gradually the clarinet confessed to higher and lower crimes, while the string players sliced and scraped with increasing appetite. The clarinet began spinning tales no rational observer could believe while the strings encouraged him to embellish further still. The strings fell into ominous unison like the chanting of a crowd, but when the clarinetist tried to plead his humble origins they erupted in renewed violence. He invented new misdeeds and transgressions and they approved vigorously. Spit trickled from the bell of the clarinet. An emboldened violinist soloed her own awesome treachery and the second violinist threatened her with retribution.

The second movement (the Larghetto) sounded as if the revolutionary spirit of the first had been encoded in a vast sluggish bureaucracy in which each instrument was required to ask permission of the others, and consequently nothing really got done. The rights to travel and free expression had been restricted. Alternatively, the victims were so spent there was no yield in torturing them more. I wondered why classical musicians almost always wear black. The cello sank an octave to demonstrate his authority over the others.

The third movement illustrated the virtues of compliance,

and I wished I were at home washing dishes. The fourth movement began as soulless propaganda before returning to the harmonious shrieks and eviscerations of the first, every performer a martyr for the cause, the suffering of the instruments a lamentable necessity. The applause was deafening.

Afterward Amanda and I got into a fight. She had found the concert uplifting. She accused me of a morbid obsession with the past, particularly the pasts of people I'd never met and the pasts of people I simply made up, and she felt that this tendency interfered with my ability to spend time meaningfully in the present with her. I pointed out that we were walking along Revolution Street toward the Jewish Quarter. The past in Prague has a way of getting in your face.

"It is impossible," she said, "to live like that; otherwise Prague would have become a heap of rubble long ago."

"That's what it is," I said, "artfully stacked rubble full of mindless creatures who sleep and eat in the sheltered bits."

"You're viewing it from Mars," she said, "and that's what I mean. It's like you're not really here."

I pointed out that where I came from people described themselves as fourth-generation Irish because it was somehow embarrassing to admit that you came from Peoria or Phoenix.

"Pasts matter," I said. "Pasts matter, because they make us who we are."

"No, actually," said Amanda, "we do that."

CARROT CLARINET

Mr. Cimarron returned from an exhibition in Vienna looking vaguely disgusted that he had sold anything. Over a drink at his suggestion he demanded that I explain why anyone would part with good money for an assemblage of car tires and telephones. I asked why anyone would make such a thing but he considered this question beneath answering. I asked how the items had been arranged or combined, and he said tastefully, of course. I asked who had purchased it and he said someone who considered it an investment likely to appreciate.

He asked what I had been up to since he discovered me. Magically he knew of a pub that served peanuts gratis. Both of us munched and smoked and sipped beer. There were risqué cartoons on the walls. He explained that under communism it was safe to portray people in and out of their underwear—there was no need to indicate profession or class or relationship to the state. Cartoons were important in an era when you could be imprisoned for photographing things in a subversive light. Moreover, not even Stalin could take away the right to make filthy jokes.

He asked if I was homesick.

"God, no," I said. "People where I'm from are damned ignorant and proud of it."

"You are the lone exception?" he said.

"Of course not. I just come from a town that is sort of stranded."

"So instead you came to a place in decline since the collapse of the Holy Roman Empire."

"I like it," I said.

"Perhaps it does not like you," he said.

"I haven't experienced active hostility," I said.

"Because you are not important. Prague despises all her inhabitants equally. It's why we all stay. We take comfort in being loathed."

"Yet she gives you beer," I said.

"You raise an excellent point as always," said Mr. Cimarron. "She'll never let anyone leave willingly. She takes comfort in spite. It's what makes Prague so appealing. Other great cities are merely indifferent."

"Or they tend toward active persecution."

"Precisely. There's hardly anywhere to sit down and smoke in New York and San Francisco."

"You travel a lot," I said.

"My installations must be installed," he said. "Sometimes I think I might prefer designing amusements for children. There could be some value in postponing their encounters with the anguish, despair, and exasperation that will characterize the rest of their lives."

Directly over our table a bald man ogled a young blonde while a fat woman behind him brandished a rolling pin. I could not really imagine Mr. Cimarron cultivating a quiet domestic life. On a far wall a woman hitched up her dress and one leg to use a urinal next to a startled man. Elsewhere there were other cartoons of a similar stripe, and perhaps if I could have read and understood the captions I would have found them funny.

Although he was cunning and disingenuous, there was an innocence to Cimarron I could not figure out. Despite his cynicism and caustic commentary about the art business, his clientele, politics, capitalism, declining standards of good manners in civil society, et cetera, these things were ultimately to him mere obstacles for a man or woman of spirit to overcome, and it was still possible to create or perceive one's own meanings despite the ongoing degradation of everything. The conversion of meaning into money caused him genuine pain, and his wish for the world to leave him alone came across as an appealing childlike petulance.

I fished for some sense of what his previous works had entailed but he wouldn't be drawn—best to forge ahead, look ahead, rest on no laurel. Though he did reminisce occasionally about the clarinet he'd made from a carrot. After coring the thing vertically he had drilled finger holes, five top and one bottom, using an electric screwdriver, and attached it to a standard mouthpiece with a B♭ reed. He'd got it right on the sixth carrot, and it played beautifully until it began to rot on the third day. When I asked what he had done for a living before his works began to sell, he surprised me. He had been a carpenter, and before that a teacher of geography. I had not thought him old enough to have had three careers. I boggled that his country withstood so many incarnations as well.

"Where are you from?" I said.

"A small village that has been dropping apples for eight hundred years."

"Not very specific."

"Emperors visit. Armies maraud nearby. An enormous cliffside castle commands a view of twenty miles in every direction. The apples continue to drop indifferently."

"Karlštejn," I said.

"Yes."

Amanda and I had visited. What both of us remembered was seeing, from the train, whole Czech families swimming and sunbathing in the river in their underwear, as though such Western fripperies as swimsuits had not yet reached the provinces, or at least that the wages that could procure them remained in Prague. The train crossed a gleaming new bridge built for tourists, not apple harvesters.

"There is nothing in the countryside but honor, and nobody can live on that," he said. "Prague as you know is the mother of cities. Shame she won't divulge paternity."

I returned home slightly buzzed and Amanda told me her godfather in England had passed away. When I asked if they had been close, she replied that she had known him for twenty-four years. She decided to take time off and return for the funeral. She told one story before she went and another when she returned.

It was an expected death, and a blessing, she said when she

first got the news. He was only eighty-one but had suffered from idiopathic pulmonary fibrosis, in which the lungs are gradually overwhelmed by scar tissue. For at least the last six months of his life he had been confined to a sofa in a back room of the family's terraced cottage near Exeter, and hooked up to an escalating intake of oxygen. He had books he didn't read and a television he didn't watch and a bell on a string he could pull when he needed attention. He had been ready to go for months. Yet Amanda's mother suggested that the only reason he hadn't unplugged himself was the fear that his wife would have no idea how to carry on. He described his illness as a bloody nuisance.

They had three grown children, each of them integral to Amanda's childhood. Despite the sad occasion Amanda was eager to see them again. I went with her to the airport on the Friday morning, simply because I enjoyed the long straight tram ride out of Prague, even though the landscape, architecture, and weather turned progressively bleaker and more ominous. Somewhere past the airport, said Amanda, the Red Army is still hanging around sniffing glue. As we rode she chattered brightly about Bob, the deceased man, Melissa, his wife, and the children: Peter, Linda, and Theo. It dawned on me as she spoke that when she talked about her childhood she was really referring to a later period involving frequent raves and occasionally fleeing from law enforcement. I took the tram back home, too. I was startled to recognize the police station where Inspector Sokol had interviewed us: one ominous block among a dozen identical, innocent blocks.

When she returned on Sunday, Amanda was pale, visibly distraught, and uncharacteristically incoherent. The funeral had gone well—a lovely commemorative service, she said. But outside the immediate family only Amanda knew the circumstances of her godfather's death.

There was no space in the sick room for the oxygen machine and its arsenal of canisters, so that was installed in a guest room with a tube conveying the oxygen through two doorways and down a hallway to the invalid. There had never been a problem with the arrangement.

When the eldest child, Peter, arrived with his American wife, his mother immediately suggested a change to his long shaggy hair, which set the tone for the rest of the visit. When Linda, the middle child, arrived she was too busy arranging her third marriage to think much about her dying father, and everyone reminded her that she had not formally terminated her second marriage yet. When baby Theo arrived it was immediately evident that he could not handle his family without getting stoned first, and whole bottles of wine went missing after everyone had gone to bed. The mother and the eldest son made futile efforts to direct the attention of the younger siblings toward the suffering and imminent demise of their father. The four of them did pass at least one tranquil hour in the living room together without Bob watching a rerun of *Father Ted*.

Amanda was closest to Peter, the eldest, who was constantly popping pills designed for people who experience panic attacks on airplanes, procured for him by his wife. Even so he whimpered in his sleep, said the wife to Amanda. She had taken him driving and giggled appreciatively at silly place names, did not count his beers, and massaged his shoulders, which she said was like kneading sheetrock. Nothing could assuage his anger, exasperation, and despair. Linda could not shut up about the new bloke and his encyclopedic knowledge of classical music. Theo passed out in the garden repeatedly. The American wife tried to help the mother in the kitchen. Peter thundered at his mother, "Every sentence out of your mouth begins with *What I do . . .*"

He slammed the hallway door on his way out, pinching the oxygen tube. Everyone's nerves were shot. Bob didn't ring his bell.

HERO

Whole districts of Prague doubled from week to week as Occupied Paris or Victorian London. Movie stars' stunt doubles could sometimes be spotted hard at work on set, while the stars themselves were rumored to be relaxing lavishly at the Four Seasons. It was said that the cost of filming in Britain or America had become horrifying even for Hollywood money.

The film sets always struck me as distillations of Prague—a place that sells fantasies to foreigners. One of the buildings in *Mission Impossible* had been SS headquarters. Fancy and reality were inextricably interwoven, and there was no real Prague where films were not made. Yet watching a given movie is like seeing Žižkov without its butterflies, and wandering Prague encountering film sets induces a burning desire to know what really happened on the spot in question. Per square yard more people may have been shot, stabbed, burned, decapitated, hanged, maimed, disemboweled, or mildly injured there than in any other European capital city.

Books set in Prague, like movies, seemed to sanitize places and misrepresent events, at least in comparison to conversations I had with Czech people. We weren't really invaded, Vlasta told me. We were betrayed by Britain and France, and a few months later there were German officers doling out chocolate to Czech children in Prague streets. Her mother thought they were very dashing. But Bohemia had probably been doomed to Western misunderstanding ever since Shakespeare gave it a coastline.

I turned a corner on my walk to work one morning and encountered, twenty feet away, a pair of uniformed SS men beneath two enormous red flags with white circles bearing swastikas draped over the façade of a beautiful baroque building of the kind too common in Prague to elicit much interest on any other day. For a fraction of a second I didn't see the film crew. I thought, conventionally enough, of Amanda, and hoped she was safe.

On another occasion the two of us had walked past a line of black cars from the '40s on a cobbled street leading to the Old Town Square, presumably there for some blockbuster I was never able to identify. A Czech police officer in contemporary uniform materialized in front of us, cocking his drawn firearm and issuing orders I didn't understand. I thought he must be an actor in a film at first, until I noticed several women bystanders moving behind their male companions as if to shield themselves if lead began flying. I turned to look for Amanda, but she had disappeared. The other bystanders began dispersing behind the police officer, who glared at me fiercely and pointed with his free hand toward an open doorway behind me. "Shut it behind you," he said in English. I found Amanda inside, halfway down a flight of stone steps leading to a cellar bar.

She said it was frightening to encounter a man with a gun and wondered what perpetrator of which crime was at loose overhead, but I was already cross with her. All the other women in the street had seemed to grab a man instinctively and all the men accepted this as their right and proper role. Amanda dived into a rabbit hole without a word. Had I been shot, I pointed out, I would have died in vain.

"It would never have occurred to me," she said. "I see no value in either of us getting shot."

"In theory," I said, "we're a unit."

"In that case," she said, "I'll let you perform your role next time. Although it's not like you to be useful."

"I just question your instincts," I said.

"Instincts," she said with a face like she was eating a wasp.

"You know, like most women in couples sleep furthest from the door."

"That's not instinct. It's manipulation. It's about who makes the coffee in the morning. Where did you hear that?"

"I don't know," I said. "Women's magazine."

"Logically," she said, "the person nearest the door should be the person who pees most often."

"That's not very romantic," I said. "And neither is your letting me get shot like a dog."

"Fine then," she said. "My romantic instincts are lacking. I have none."

"Well, can you pretend occasionally?"

"Would you like the wedding photos in sepia?"

"We're getting married?" I said.

"Could help with visas," she said. "And I could use a new surname." She had always felt cursed as a Smith.

NIL NISI RECTUM

The motto of the House of Schwarzenberg is NIL NISI REC-TUM, which sadly does not translate from the Latin into *Nothing but ass*. Sixty miles east of Prague stands a structure universally known to English speakers as the Bone Church or the Church of Bones, in which the Schwarzenberg coat of arms with its motto hangs on one wall, crafted from tibias and fibulas and skulls. Nearly everything else in the church is also fashioned from human remains. An enormous chandelier featuring at least one of every bone in the human body hangs from the ceiling, and there are four immense bell-shaped mounds of skulls. The origins of the Bone Church according to Ivan were that, first, someone brought back some dirt from the Holy Land, and wealthy locals demanded to be buried in it. Later it was discovered to be profitable to disinter the wealthy bones

and sell the burial dirt to even wealthier subsequent generations. Genteel bones began to accumulate in a corner of the
church. Whereon the Black Death struck in 1348, and bones
of all manner of lifestyle, profession, and socioeconomic strata
joined in. It became the world's most ecumenical congregation.
In 1860 an artist named František Rint—his name is spelled in
phalanges and metacarpals on the south wall, with vertebrae for
punctuation—strapped, perhaps, for cash to buy paint or other
orthodox art supplies, got to work creating a magnificent and
macabre work of bricolage. Peering through a grate in the back
of the Bone Church you could see the contributions of recent
delinquents: beer cans, candy wrappers, and spent Marlboros
on a sprawling bed of pelvises, coccyges, patellae, and skulls.

I had a new gig. I was sent once a week to teach tobacco
executives at a sparkling new factory fifty steps away from the
ossuary. By comparison to the factory, the Bone Church was
quite normal. The factory's administration was housed in a
seventeenth-century Cistercian monastery complex, and all
the purveyors of lung cancer, emphysema, and so on rubbed
shoulders beneath beautifully preserved frescoes of various
saints being decapitated or disemboweled. The centerpiece
in the former mess hall was a bishop wandering over hill and
down dale with his mitered severed head clutched to his belly.
Cigarette production was handled by a small army of ghosts—a
hypothesis I could test, my students told me, by looking for live
humans doing actual work.

The Cistercians, they said, were ultimately banned from
Czech lands for cruelty surpassing that of the Jesuits. Legend
held that once a month a local virgin was required to deliver
provisions to the monastery. Recent archaeological excavations
had uncovered the remains of several young women.

I taught the director of Corporate Social Responsibility, a voluptuous redhead in her early forties whom I found very distracting. She was nearly as tall as I, which suggested both a personal challenge and a conspiracy between us against the lesser people. She was also very smart and very impatient. She already knew how to say that a twelve-year-old who takes up smoking a pack a day is worth $75,000 to the company over the course of a lifetime. She and the global corporation broadly were under enormous pressure to provide something else to the twelve-year-old beyond occasional moments of inner peace and a lifetime of health complications. The conservation of the monastery was just a starting point.

"It is common," said Director Šarka, "in Kutná Hora for someone to go to the basement for potatoes only to find that the basement has fallen fifty yards into a medieval silver mine, and all the potatoes with it. Last week I ordered eight million dollars' worth of cement. We want to keep the houses aboveground."

Eighteen international geologists—called the UNESCO Working Group on Land Subsidence—had studied and considered the ways that monuments, heritage buildings, storied dungeons, and whole cities like Kutná Hora could collapse into a bubble of subterranean air without some timely intervention. Accordingly the Swiss cheese earth beneath Kutná Hora was stabilized by pouring concrete into holes. Since the extent of underground perforation was not known the volume of concrete required was also unclear, and the plan evidently was to keep pouring until the concrete was level with the open-air surface.

I became very nervous just walking around in Kutná Hora. Mostly I tried to teach Šarka how to read UNESCO guidelines, demoralizing for both of us because impossible. Kutná Hora once rivaled Prague for wealth and splendor, and is a World Heritage site. Therefore concrete can be poured into holes only in specific and highly restricted ways.

In Kutná Hora there was a fourteenth-century cathedral resembling a spaceship, a whole district of homes with gables and turrets and oriels dating from the Renaissance, and a very pleasant town square for people watching. Kutná Hora is also the source of all evil. The first thalers were minted there, and in time came to be called *dollars.*

Šarka belonged to a strange internal corporate entity called the Smoking Board, people from various tobacco companies around the world who could take two puffs of a given tobacco and identify it as Turkish, 1997, then argue amongst themselves whether it was coastal or Anatolian highland in origin. A few times a year this group convened around a mound of palate-cleansing parsley to try new products and deliberate over multimillion-dollar questions like whether to market the new product to women or children.

"You belong to the illuminati," I said.

"Actually," she said, "a lot of our input just gets ignored. Making better cigarettes is too expensive. Instead they change the size of the filter and sell the usual stuff in different packaging. Greek smokers won't buy something that says *Turkish* on the label. American smokers like the word *American.* I think they are very insecure. We try to appeal to women and upper-class smokers everywhere with terms like *domestic blend.*"

"Do you ever," I said, "do anything normal for work? Like type a memo?"

"Every day," she said. "But you are in luck. The Board's next meeting is here in Kutná Hora. Our meetings are confidential but our social hours are not."

.   .   .

Amanda looked fabulous in combat boots and paramilitary gear—Šarka told us to dress for mud. Amanda came for a change from her usual routine. In our teaching trajectories and our relationship we were like king and queen, and I could only falter one step in any direction while she surveyed the chessboard with scope and range and power. My role was to observe and be grateful and stick to a safe position.

Šarka sported a fetching black beret. The other six board members were similarly tricked out in olive drab or black when we met in an orchard outside Kutná Hora at first light, like commandos behind the lines without insignia. There were two bulky Pavels, one Polish and one Russian. There was an amiable Canadian named Dave and an agile Mauritanian called Ismail. A towering Samoan called Iulio stood next to a short Italian woman named Delia who looked more like a hostage than a committed volunteer.

Our mission was to find a waterwheel—a rare carnivorous plant—so that they could smoke it. There was no commercial value in the enterprise, but it was a ceremonial ritual for them to find something indigenous wherever they met and create cocktail cigarettes to commemorate the occasion. They were probably the only people in the world who could distinguish between a cigarette containing the waterwheel plant and any other. They were searching for that particular item because the rarer and more localized the plant, the better.

As the name suggests, the waterwheel is aquatic. Our first objective was the stream at the bottom of the orchard. Šarka had a map in a laminated cover. There were numerous intersecting waterways nearby. Nobody had ever seen a waterwheel, but Šarka had a picture on a page ripped from a Czech encyclopedia, and photocopies for each of us. She also had water bottles and rain gear for me and Amanda, and she carried a portable hair dryer. You don't get authorized to spend eight million bucks for nothing. She slung it from one hip like a sidearm.

I asked Polish Pavel about previous expeditions. He told me that in New York one autumn they had smoked the leaves of American elms they gathered in Central Park. In Berlin they smoked linden leaves under some linden trees. Rome was more fun, because they infiltrated the Vatican City gardens with scissors and filched several roses. He had not been on any other missions because he was the junior recruit.

It was usually best to smoke flowers—not for the taste, but for the symbolism. We were looking for the waterwheel's small white blossoms, afloat in shallow but swift and clear water. If we spotted the plant, confirmation should be simple: the waterwheel is one of the fastest-moving plants in the world, closing its traps even quicker than a Venus flytrap despite the extra burden of running water. Essentially we planned to spend the day tickling vegetation to see if it attacked.

"What do you suppose it eats?" I said to Polish Pavel as we walked. "Tadpoles?"

"Maybe alligators."

"That explains why there are no alligators in Central Europe. They've been cleansed."

"Now the waterwheel needs a new food source," he said.

"Foreigners go missing in Czech countryside," I said.

"Rescue teams vanish," he said.

"NATO forces overwhelmed," I said.

"Evolution accelerates," he said.

"The speed of light decelerates," I said.

"Pots of gold are no longer attached to rainbows," he said.

"Oh, come on."

"Look," he said, pointing. A bright orange and black sala-mander scurried away from us into the stream. It had not been devoured by a plant. We had lost the others, and no one else saw it.

The bank opposite the orchard was on a slope layered in pine needles. Pavel thought the acid from the pine needles might dis-courage things from growing or living nearby or downstream. Upstream looked promising.

We spun out still sillier apocalyptic scenarios as we walked. Y2K was around the corner. We talked about sports, and how extravagantly satisfying it had been to watch the Czechs humili-ate Russia on ice for the hockey gold at the Nagano Olympics. Earlier that year France had hosted and won the World Cup with tremendous flair. Pavel suggested that more Czech and French babies had been conceived afterward than in any other year since 1945. We hardly noticed the rain as it transitioned from mist to drizzle, but downpour got our attention. We kept mostly under trees as we walked, still scanning the stream for white flowers, but the rain changed again into a malevolent entity, a grey regime interrogating every exposed surface and infiltrating my shoes. Thunder threatened us from somewhere nearby and Pavel pointed to the opening of a small cave.

The putrefaction was overwhelming even before we entered and both of us pinched our noses. We had to stoop because the opening was just tall enough for—I guessed—a medieval silver miner. Lightning struck nearby—we were safer in than out. We moved forward crouching, Pavel in the lead. With a thin click of his Zippo we had a modicum of light.

Ten feet in we came to a wall of new concrete, and against it a huge lump of decomposing fur beneath a cloud of flies. In the flickering light I could make out only powerful shoulders, short legs ending in plump toes, and a globe of a belly swarming with white or grey maggots. Pavel identified it as a wild boar. Stained blood on the wall and disturbed earth beneath it suggested he had given both a pretty hard time before he succumbed, attacking them as if something of value lay on the other side.

We retreated to the entrance, still pinching our noses and trying not to retch until it was safe. Then we moved to stand under a tree instead. Pavel offered me a cigarette and lit mine before his.

"I hate my Zippo," he said. "I always taste the fuel."

As planned we mustered in the orchard at noon. At first it was a joyful scene: Šarka had gone to the car and returned with beer and baguettes and meat and cheese and a picnic blanket. Everyone was decked out in mud and soaked through. But Ismail had found a cluster of waterwheels—eight of them were laid out to dry on the blanket, side by side, each about six inches long and looking like rosemary. We were unable to admire the plants' hunting prowess since the traps had closed upon harvesting. Dave the Canadian described hilariously how Russian Pavel had cleaned a whole muddy hillside with his ass. Italian Delia had a hot date with a lonely beer. Amanda and Šarka appeared to be fast friends, tapping each other's arms as they spoke.

I told our story. Nobody knew anything about boars except where to order the tasty kind. Jokes were made, but Šarka's face crumpled.

"We were careful about bats," she said.

UNESCO's chief concern lay in preserving views that glorified humanity; they stipulated streetlight placement to the millimeter. Šarka's chief concern was doing what UNESCO told her to. The cement had been poured from above with only temporary braces erected within possible exits like our cave. There was no environmental auditor of Kutná Hora conservation. Šarka was unlikely to face consequences, at least.

Delicate diplomacy ensued. Russian Pavel applied Šarka's portable hair dryer to the waterwheel plants and proposed that we smoke them in tribute to the boar, a mighty warrior who scoffed at death. Šarka thought he wasn't taking things seriously enough. Delia thought that if they could end the stupid ritual now she wouldn't have to get up at 5:00 a.m. next time. Polish Pavel argued that tradition must be maintained and that Russian Pavel's proposal was the thoughtful way to do it. Amanda chipped in to say that she would smoke or abstain at Šarka's suggestion. Even though she wasn't even a member of the Board.

Solidarity or beer ultimately prevailed, and Šarka rolled a spliff. Amanda seemed to love it. To me it tasted like any other cigarette.

STANDING RULE

Amanda looked like azaleas in May and she spoke like the BBC World Service. While I still held court at the bar of the Golden Lion, she now had students who referred to themselves as clients. Amanda's clients were lawyers overseeing the expropriation of wealth, or finding creative ways for wealth to misbehave, or alleviating the suffering inflicted on wealth by the shocking and abhorrent practice of taxation. They gave her gifts and bottles of wine, and she came home more than once in somebody's Porsche, but never the same Porsche twice, which I thought very considerate.

We envied each other. She would have enjoyed a pint with my students, and I wanted to play weekend paintball with the lads.

One of her many talents was to go to any restaurant in Prague, take three bites of any dish, and say that she could do better at home. Two or three days later, she did. In contrast, when I cooked she complained that I couldn't really expect her to regard sautéed potatoes as a main course, or that I had clearly mistaken a cup of salt for the cup of sugar the recipe called for. Somehow we ate well anyway. After washing up we took to the sofa or bathtub with books unless there was a movie in English with Czech dubbing on television, and by some strange accident we watched a lot of Clint Eastwood movies in German. At one point President Clinton appeared on the screen with a Czech voiceover.

"It's clear," said Amanda, "that he is saying the villagers have run out of food and the wolves are beginning to howl and tall dark masts have appeared on the horizon. Yet I have no idea what he's talking about."

Some weekends we would go to the main train station to catch the first departure to anywhere but Auschwitz, Amanda's standing rule. A year on and we were mildly irritated and bored with Prague, with Graceland, and perhaps with each other. We disembarked at whim, visited the nearest castle or cathedral if we found it, ate Czech pub grub, always mysteriously superior in the provinces, and took a late train back to Prague or stayed somewhere if we felt like it. The fountain in Mariánské Lázně ejaculates and none of the elderly German tourists seem to find it funny. The Egon Schiele museum in Český Krumlov meant more to Amanda than to me. I can't remember the name of the place where we accidentally stayed in a brothel.

It was a town of brick buildings so tall and narrow they seemed to shiver in the winter cold, each with high gables concealing some dark secret or creature of dubious origin, and the streets were deserted but the alleys bustled. We did not explore much, because in the center of town we found a small park with a steep slope and half a dozen Czech children zooming down it on plastic sleds.

"I think I have a shopping bag," said Amanda.

"So?"

She gave me the same look she once gave me for asking if the tide came in at the same time each day. I grew up a thousand miles from the sea and five hundred miles from a really good hill. She took her toiletries out of a plastic shopping bag and dumped them into her rucksack, which she handed to me. Then she sat on her bag and went down the hill as fast as a sneeze, with three heads and five arms and nine legs.

Every Czech child stopped to gape in envy.

She trudged back up the hill with a triumphant smile contested by a serious giggle. She invited me to check the rucksack for another bag, and she set off again to demonstrate improvisational luge. I did find a bag, and when I sat on it my prefrontal cortex was flooded with dopamine and adrenaline. My lumbar vertebrae had some reservations. As I was climbing the hill again I felt sorry for the children proceeding at such safe and stately speeds aboard their high-tech sliders. Amanda took pity on one especially pathetic specimen and offered her the bag. She squealed in gleeful terror all the way down.

Two or three runs later a burly woman was waiting for us at the top of the hill.

"This place is for children," she said in English, and stomped away before we could reply.

"I'm sure she can't do that," I said.

"I'm sure she just did," said Amanda.

An older boy came through the park gate with a whole flotilla of carrier bags held high in one hand. He distributed them to all of his friends, and Amanda's own improbable revolution slid raucously downhill. The woman who had discouraged us glared ferociously. We joined the kids.

When we limped eventually from the field we were in dire need of a pub, and the first we came to had two empty easy chairs next to a fireplace. We both ordered grog and draped our wet socks over the iron grate surrounding the fire and aimed our toes at it. From her rucksack Amanda produced a pen and a postcard and asked why I never wrote to my mother.

"We talk on the phone," I said. At the time that meant finding a pay phone far from a tram line and speaking quickly.

"She writes to you," she said. She put her parents' address on the postcard. I tried to think of anything I hadn't reported home by phone but couldn't. I made the mistake of saying so.

"You could always tell her how much you drink," said Amanda. "She'd love that."

"Are you mad?"

"British mad or American mad?"

"Well, you're not being American nice."

"I'm not American."

By that time we had already had several stupid arguments with no discernible cause or purpose.

"You're hardly teetotal," I said.

"You said something really pretentious the day we met about preferring the conversational culture of Europe. You meant that you like to sit around in pubs and bars drinking."

"I also drink at home."

"I barely noticed."

Eventually when she had scribbled the correct cheerful and meaningless message on her postcard she got up to fetch us more drinks in her bare feet. When after fifteen minutes she failed to reappear, I went to investigate.

Amanda was standing at the bar in an adjoining room talking to another man. She gave me a bright hello and a lukewarm grog. He gave me a withering scowl.

"This is Dave," she said. "His girlfriend Valerie has just popped to the ladies'. They are fugitives from Hotel Doom, though they have only recently escaped."

Dave was a thin Australian, surprisingly short when he stepped down from his barstool. Valerie, when she appeared, was a woman from Iowa a head taller than he even without her messy black curls that were determined not to comply with gravity. We colonized a table near a window after I had gone to fetch our wet things.

Dave lost no time explaining that he had escaped English teaching by landing a job as a business reporter for *The Prague Post,* a handsome English-language weekly broadsheet with a circulation of thirty thousand. He investigated things like the municipal construction contracts in Prague that all went mysteriously to one French company. He sounded very prosecutorial about it. Valerie did proofreading for an international law firm, which was, she said, amazingly even less interesting than it sounded, but the pay spared her from enduring Doom. Dave bought the next round condescendingly because we were still teachers.

Valerie had glasses pushed up into her hair, the high widow's peak on her forehead making her look dazzlingly intellectual. She had prominent cheekbones and a jutting chin, yet looked somehow soft and receptive, except that she also looked deeply skeptical and often giggled to herself as if someone had said something stupid, or laughed at her own jokes before she had finished making them. Her dark brown eyes were somehow opaque, as though it were impossible to get in there.

Foolishly I mentioned the Smoking Board.

"Exactly what does this Smoking Board do?" said Dave, reportorially.

"It's just like a focus group," I said.

"What do they focus on?"

"My student explained the other day how the feminization of smoking never happened behind the iron curtain, because feminism didn't happen."

"So no Vagina Slimes," said Valerie.

"I beg your pardon?" said Amanda.

"Virginia Slims," I said, "an American cigarette brand for women."

"You've come a long way, baby," said Valerie.

"Right. So the board talks about things like how to introduce fashion cigarettes in Central and Eastern Europe."

"They have a marketing department for that," said Dave.

"Surely it isn't difficult," said Valerie. "Make the cigarettes slimmer with a pink stripe."

"They don't smoke full-time," said Amanda. "They have other normal jobs."

"It sounds like a secret cabal within a sinister corporation," said Dave.

"It's just people going to work every day," I said.

"Actually," said Dave, "a significant number of women snipers and fighter pilots hold or held the Soviet medal of honor."

"You say that like it's a good thing," said Valerie. "You could kill people but you couldn't go to med school or law school."

"Of course," said Amanda. "You work with lawyers now."

"Every woman working there is under thirty except the German brass," said Valerie.

"Maybe the male workforce was so depleted by war the

women had a reproductive deficit to pay off," I suggested. "Now, comrades: four each."

"Well," said Valerie, "Russian women went to work in 1917. All of 'em. Other places, other dates, same policy. It's why they still don't like feminism. They got the Vladimir Lenin edition."

"I very much doubt," said Dave, "that your Russian sisters all clocked in at 8:00 a.m. on the first day of Red October."

"My sister is from Davenport," said Valerie.

"How many members of this Smoking Board are there, and how often do they meet?" said Dave to me.

"Moreover," said Valerie, "the reason for your sexy Soviet warrior women is that it was important to stay blue collar, particularly if you had children. Education was dangerous."

"I'd like to pursue this story," said Dave. I did not like the sound of Šarka turning into a story.

"Furthermore," said Valerie.

"Jesus Christ," said Dave.

"Furthermore," said Valerie, "I can't help wondering why you're surprised that women can shoot straight and fly well."

"Well, historically," said Dave.

"They weren't asked," said Valerie.

"Are you done yet?" said Dave.

"Done with what?" said Valerie.

"You are arguing with me for no reason in front of other people," said Dave. He stood up and walked out. Valerie snorted with exasperation, shrugged for our benefit, and followed him.

"I like her," said Amanda.

We finished their drinks when it was clear they weren't returning. We ordered chicken that we were obliged to barrage with salt, necessitating more beer, and we agreed on a Becherovka nightcap. Amanda found in her British guidebook an apparently respectable place to stay just five minutes' walk away, although in retrospect I'm sure it had not been inspected.

At the reception desk sat a bald bored bespectacled man of middle age. Convivial sounds emanated from an adjoining lounge, but we didn't go there. We were tired, drunk, and foreign. The man slid our key wordlessly over his desk and pointed to the stairway. We went upstairs, got undressed, brushed our teeth, and Amanda was already asleep while I was still flossing.

When I woke up, Amanda said that at first she had thought she was at Graceland. There was a polar bear rug and a Dalí love seat shaped like lips and a mirror wall. We had slept beneath pink sheets on pink pillows under a bright red duvet, but it all seemed at first no more than a reflection of someone's eccentric taste. Amanda suggested that we hurry so we could catch breakfast—it was late.

There was no sound in the corridor and almost all the doors were open, all the rooms similarly decorated—just a strange boutique hotel out of season. There was no one at the reception desk and no smell of coffee or sound of silverware.

In the lounge we had not seen the previous night several photo albums sat on various tables. Amanda opened one to find captioned Polaroid photos of mostly young women. Some of the Czech words we understood included *Russian, Ukrainian, African,* and *Thai.* It dawned on us both that the place was a brothel. Amanda shut the book and turned to me.

"I don't think they do breakfast here," she said.

MAP OF PRAGUE

Šarka was duly harassed by a *Prague Post* reporter who claimed to have sensitive information about the Smoking Board, though he didn't. Šarka was in turn instructed to find a new English teacher, someone who showed more discretion and was less likely to prove a liability in a business environment. I couldn't fathom the force of imagination required to describe the factory thus. More important, my hours were not replaced and I was no longer in good standing with my employer, a teaching agency that placed me in various jobs. Ivan, Milan, and Vlasta swore sideways that they were happy with their tuition, and I continued with them, but I was not earning enough to live on, and I was heavily reliant on Amanda. Worse still, the *Prague Post* did run an article skeptical of Big Tobacco's extensive philanthropic activities, and I worried they might stop pouring concrete.

There were scores of job advertisements in the *Post* each week, largely because recent graduates in a faraway place with no workplace regulation count as cheap labor. I could find work stuffing envelopes, entering data, collating documents, punching holes, answering telephones, or replying to customer complaints, and none of it was likely to yield a living wage. Alternatively I could probably wrap bagels or pour beer for tourists. New language schools opened daily, but I didn't want to teach anymore.

My employment experience consisted, roughly, of getting stoned with my manager at an Indiana pizza parlor, then locking up and playing Frisbee in the street on slow days; opening boxes of new acquisitions at the university library, but mostly just reading them; loading and unloading dishwashers; restocking frozen foods on the night shift at a local grocery store; and occasional summer gardening work for my viciously sociopathic former elementary school music teacher. Worse, I had nothing to show for my time in Prague, no skills or experience to save me from waiting tables in double shifts while struggling to pay the rent if I returned home or went elsewhere. During my underemployed phase I sometimes went shopping for carrots and onions and got hit by a wave of despair. Safer to remain at home on the sofa, except that every evening Amanda asked what I had done that day.

I had a series of humiliating job interviews, like bungled medical examinations. The interviewer or interviewers determined that I was unfit for purpose by asking stupid invasive questions, as though nobody understood that nobody is fit for purpose but everyone must pay rent. I failed repeatedly to show passion, dedication, and enthusiasm over teamwork, time management, and problem-solving. I felt that the people interviewing me could recognize neither a clock nor a correct answer.

The first rule of any language, I thought, is that actions speak louder than words. I met a lot of self-important, disorganized prospective employers.

Eventually I had an interview with Terence, who asked how fast I could type and told me to prove it. I started work the next day as a kind of amanuensis in his translation agency. A bilingual Czech woman named Hana dictated while I typed and corrected on the fly. We each got about a penny per word, and we were fast. Terence was a Harvard-educated scion of some dynasty from the U.S. Northeast that reliably produced Democratic congressmen and millionaires, but he was content running his own business in a Prague hovel, getting stoned before breakfast and drunk before lunch while hurling abuse at his wife, his employees, his clients, and his cat, Merunka, which means "apricot" in Czech. He must have harbored some private trauma. I was spared performance reviews and internal e-mails.

I got to know Prague in novel ways. If there were changes in civic administration or traffic regulation we translated something about it, along with countless leases, deeds, press releases, and contracts. I learned in detail if not in advance about scores of arrests and indictments. Coincidentally Amanda started bringing home reports and articles and draft speeches that she corrected for her clients. Her homework had international scope: most of it corresponded somehow to the expansion of the European Union. Sometimes I helped her on weekends, sitting at a sidewalk café on Parížska Street. I said we were just like Sartre and de Beauvoir and she snorted. She worked and wasn't sure what I did all day. She'd take philosophy over business waffle in a heartbeat, she said.

Employed, I felt even more lonely and isolated. Hana and I were tired of each other by the end of each day, and socializing with Terence was a terrible mistake most of the time, depending upon which conspiracy theory he had embraced that week. Once in a while he was almost charming, when reminiscing about a summer spent painting houses and getting stoned in Maine, eating his weight in lobsters and ice cream. Other times he was morose about his tenure in the CIA, FBI, NSA, Military Intelligence, or all four—counting Soviet tanks on the East German border, or listening to Russian voices from the back of a van in East Berlin. His details were interchangeable. His thesis was that he was a war hero. Perhaps he was and could not therefore tell any truths. On the other hand, he was ferociously intelligent, doing crosswords in Hungarian for fun while getting drunk in the mornings.

Terence's flat was in a small menacing square in the Old Town, ten minutes' walk from Graceland. Once a week I was dispatched to buy coffee and snacks for the whole office, which I enjoyed even though it cut into my earnings, and Hana's, too. Directly across the square behind a wall that never encountered direct sunlight was a law firm. I had seen Valerie coming and going half a dozen times before I recognized her. We compared notes one lunch hour and decided our jobs were very similar. Over lunch the following week she suggested that together we could probably draw a map of Prague showing the net worth of notable residents plus who was sleeping with whom. On Fridays Amanda joined us after work for drinks in an expat bar called La Casa Blů. Dave never showed and Valerie didn't talk about him much.

I said one Friday that there was a problem with Valerie's proposed map of Prague, an omission. Amanda rolled her eyes. I tried to tell her about my recent discovery of an item in an American newspaper about a Czech silver medalist who had recently died in a Galveston nursing home. She was survived by three children and eight grandchildren. Her husband had passed away two years previously. No mention was made of her toes, although it was noted that she had emigrated in 1968, as if this were a commonplace occurrence. I was sure that I could do a better job of reporting than that, and I wondered how or if Czech newspapers covered her death. I learned that she was born and raised in Kutná Hora, and that in later life she became a goldsmith.

But Amanda wasn't interested. On this and other things, she said, the world had moved on except for me.

I told Valerie and she promised to ask someone at work how they would go about determining the identity of our former neighbor. There was surely a property register at the very least, an electoral roll, some footprint.

She came up short on those things. The apartment building had until recently belonged to a collective whose individual members' names were not recorded. But Valerie also brought with her a huge and horrifying brochure. Unknown to us the building had been purchased by a developer who envisioned it entirely renovated and filled with IKEA flat pack beds for tourists to sleep on. The courtyard might get flowers and a fountain. The roof would be retiled with Australian terra-cotta.

SOVIET SQUIRRELS

Mr. Cimarron made a series of large objects out of real hammers and real sickles. The wooden shafts of the hammers could be aligned as a platform, wall, or roof, with the hammer heads on alternating sides. The sickles served as adornments and two sickles facing each other formed apertures of adjustable size. When I asked him what they were for he said birds.

"Don't you think they might injure themselves on the blades?" I said. I had stopped by his studio unheralded and unannounced.

"When is the last time you used a sickle?" he said.

"Never."

"Exactly. They haven't been sharpened for several decades."

"And you are confident that a bird is going to want to live in one of these things."

"Not necessarily a birdhouse. A bird study. A trysting place."

"I'm sure they have some artistic merit," I said, "but I'll be surprised if your birds appreciate it."

"Look at this one," he said, holding aloft a kind of large spider with a wooden abdomen and six curved pointy legs. "And pretend you're a squirrel."

Put that way, each object looked eminently purposeful and effective. The blades didn't need to be sharp.

"It's not like you to make something useful," I said.

"It pains me," he said. "But at least I am not helping people."

"Where do you propose to hang them?" I said.

"That is the real dishonor," he said. "This is commissioned work. I must hang them where I am told to hang them. My client owns a hotel outside Prague with extensive gardens on a sensitive migration route."

"You're building rest stops between Kenya and Norway."

"I should export," he said. "Also effective against lions and tigers. Would you like to help me install them? John Steinbeck once stayed there."

The hotel was more of a complex, almost a village, in the mountains, with air so clear and pure I felt dizzy walking through gardens filled with marble and white limestone statues of great men—Marx, Wittgenstein, Beethoven—that lined gravel paths and supervised the cultivation of roses. I didn't think the Great Men likely to appreciate Mr. Cimarron's ironic contraptions. He had parked the car and gone looking for the hotelier in one of several large colonnaded buildings. There were couples and families taking pictures—evidently Marx with bunny ears never fails—but nobody around who looked like a guest. It struck me that the place was less hotel than international conference center with nothing currently on.

Mr. Cimarron emerged and said that he could not find his client or anyone else. We tried the door of another colonnaded building and it opened. Inside we found a vast empty lounge full of antique furniture, with flocked wallpaper depicting fanciful birds and a stopped clock on a black marble base on the mantel over a feeble fire. Through another door we came to a large library consisting only of books with leather spines, with rows of standing desks on which monks would copy manuscripts—at least, it wasn't a library that anyone would know how to use now. A stack of thick leather-bound ledgers contained on inspection records of train arrivals and departures.

In a third building we found a disconcertingly modern kitchen with a phalanx of pint glasses still drying upside down on a towel next to the dishwasher, but it was not obvious who put them there. An adjacent dining room was not so much modern as modernist: polished granite floors and midcentury furniture. A three-hour dinner there would evoke all the anxieties of the age, starting with back pain.

"Surely," I said, "there is a sign that says *Reception* somewhere, and a receptionist sitting under it."

"You Americans will make everything unfit for human habitation eventually," said Mr. Cimarron.

"Well, there must be a gardener."

"It's good to be out of Prague," he said. "Every inch drenched in blood and steeped in alchemy, with a whiff of Soviet body odor."

"You should write for Lonely Planet," I said.

When we finally found a gardener she told Mr. Cimarron in Czech that the hotelier had been arrested and taken away in a dawn raid. The police themselves had lingered until just before we arrived, interviewing staff and dismissing them one by one. She had stayed on because there was quite a bit of pruning to get through.

"Well, did she say why he was arrested?" I said.

"Possession of excess money," he said.

"Anything a little more specific?"

"The problem is that I meant to claim some of the excess money in return for your hard work."

"I haven't done anything."

"You're about to. I don't have room for these things. Where shall we hang them?"

"I don't know. Are we talking storks or warblers here?"

"I think we can rule out emus. Otherwise I have no idea."

We explored the grounds further—or at least an arboretum, a wildlife refuge, a lake, and a tennis court. On the surface of the tennis court I found a piece of paper. It was the itinerary for an annual convention of diabetes researchers concluded the previous month.

"Let's go back to the wildlife refuge," said Mr. Cimarron.

"What do you know about your client?" I said.

"He's very fat," said Mr. Cimarron.

"Do you have any helpful information?"

"He uses a wheelchair," he said. "And a loud whistle to summon his staff."

"We can probably eliminate violent crime," I said.

"If I'm not mistaken he was a lawyer or a professor or both. Ah, and the hotel was confiscated from his family in 1948. Later he crossed some line and got volunteered for the steelworks."

"Jolly."

"Well, it was. You joked with all the doctors and judges and dissidents around you, and steel was the last thing you thought about. I think this is how he lost the use of his legs. Still preferable to the uranium mines."

"So he didn't rob a bank."

"Keen on wildlife. Hence the preserve and the bird feeders," he said.

"But corrupt."

"I don't know. There are only two ways to make money: crime and exploitation. The rest of us just cover our expenses."

"I don't think he was exploiting the diabetes researchers, do you?"

"I'm sure their employers do that," he said.

The man in question had done marvelous work with his wildlife refuge. Split log fencing and screens of trees divided it into microhabitats; there were egrets in a marshy area and corncrakes nesting in a newly mown field with signs in Czech, German, and English explaining these things. We could also expect deer, fox, wild boar, and, most thrillingly, European lynx if we knew where and how to look. Tall trees obscured or revealed a distinctly Czech sun rolling through the sky like a lopped-off head; a bird of prey wheeled beneath it looking for something fragile to terminate.

"It will probably be in the papers tomorrow," said Mr. Cimarron.

He selected some climbable trees on the edge of a small meadow and produced some lengths of chain. I gave him a boost up; he was nearly weightless. We hung all six Soviet anti-squirrel devices but did not fill them since we didn't know what with and didn't have any anyway. Back in the first building Mr. Cimarron had tried he left a note in what looked like a standard, non-fancy office, with a desk and a chair and a telephone, but all the filing cabinets were ajar and the files missing.

Incidents involving molten metal, said Ivan the following day, are almost always fatal, for the simple reason that molten metal rarely travels in small quantities; if several tons of dry sand or anything else dropped onto a person the result would be the same as with an equal weight of liquid steel, although the temperature involved, 2,500 degrees Fahrenheit, might yield some other symptoms. The explosions common at steelworks, he continued, varied in damage mostly according to ventilation. He had investigated several. Harmless explosions in open spaces occurred daily. Ivan didn't think the hotelier had lost the use of his legs to mere burns. The likeliest explanation in Ivan's opinion as he read and translated the newspaper for me was that the man had been involved in some unspecified crushing accident on-site decades previously.

After the revolution the man became one of several investors who used government money to purchase government shares in the steelworks, after which it was mismanaged into the ground. A great foundry of bridges and battleships, an icon of Czech industry and ingenuity, an employer of generations—its blast furnaces lay cold, its ladles sold or scrapped, its rail spurs derelict.

"Is there any mention of the hotel?" I said.

"No," said Ivan.

"Well, he avenged himself beautifully."

VELIKONOCE

Shopping in the Christmas market that November, a woman nearby said, "Blow job?" I said, "Pardon?" Amanda steered me by the elbow toward some decorative eggs, while suggesting that I learn to identify a sales pitch.

Preparations for Czech Christmas were always absorbing but the prospect of experiencing Czech Christmas wasn't. Large blue plastic tubs appeared on street corners, and you could get the huge carp inside decapitated while you waited, or let it live in your bath until the appointed hour. Prague gutters ran with bloody water, like, said Amanda, lambs' blood in Greek sewers at Easter. Many Czech Christmas traditions seemed devoted to predicting who in the family would die in the coming year. The others predicted who would or would not get married. Few of these traditions were observed strictly anymore, but I had the impression that historically Czech Christmas was a time of terror and tears.

During the previous Christmas I had returned to the United States and Amanda to the UK; spending the holidays together felt like some rite of passage we had inexplicably skipped before. Amanda suggested and I agreed that we might get bored, just the two of us. Like surreptitious heathens, we went looking for a large ham. We invited other expats for dinner as Christmas carp refugees. As if by accident we discovered that we were going to have eight guests at Graceland. We bought a second ham.

The only guests I knew were Dave and Valerie. The others were Amanda's. At the last minute I realized that if we were going to be loud we had better invite Sonja, too. Amanda thought our neighbor would surely be returning to Germany, but I discovered that instead she had laid in enough alcohol to get through the week alone in a coma.

Amanda wanted to do something traditional, but I argued that we should do something American, like boil the ham in eight liters of Coca-Cola. I also made corn bread in three varieties—Mild, Hell, and Texas—mixed some bacon with some green beans, and mashed sweet potatoes with brown sugar and orange juice, melting a few marshmallows on top. The last dish aroused suspicion. The chief problem was that it was the same color as Christmas carp.

Dinner conversation was full of lively speculation on the scriptural justification for eating carp. Fish was symbolically important in Christianity, of course, but the choice of a bottom-feeder was unusual. Sonja pointed out that carp is also theoretically served on Christmas Eve in Germany, but that she didn't know anybody who ate it. Valerie suggested that loving the lowest, humblest, and most mud- and crap-filled of fishes might be the most Christian of all gestures. Surely Czech Jesus would see through our airs and pretentiousness and admonish us for enjoying such a delicious ham.

Amanda had decorated a small plastic tree with state-issued ornaments from the '80s she'd found in a flea market. They were avidly secular and symbolically meaningless glass baubles, but she had folded a thousand-crown note into a Star of David and placed it on top for good cheer. With Sonja's help we had made a festive drinks tray.

Nearly all of us had begun as teachers of English in Prague, yet each of us had drifted into work better paid, less stable, and less obviously conducive to building a career trajectory of accumulated expertise that could be applied at subsequent stages. Rivers of paperwork required drafting and proofreading in English for the European Union to annex Central Europe, and the concurrent expansion of NATO also demanded herculean administration. We were all froth on a wave of international ink spilled by Czech diplomats, lawyers, economists, politicians, and military men, and we were collectively aware that when the wave crested we would scatter, perhaps surfacing elsewhere as some smaller more isolated thing.

In addition to Dave's newspaper, Valerie's law firm, my translation agency, and Amanda's ministries, we had a guest who worked on developing international study programs, and another whose work involved turning Prague into an international conference center on par with Vienna, and a professional freelance translator of literary fiction. Somehow as an actual EU bureaucrat Sonja became the high priestess of the table.

Her work was inherently dull and absurd, to do with the welfare of working animals in developing countries, but she had a deep and unshakeable faith in bureaucracy.

"Well," said Valerie, "is a carp a working animal?" Valerie wore a green sweater over red jeans and the rest of us looked dim and disengaged by comparison.

"I work for the benefit of donkeys and horses," said Sonja, patiently, as if Valerie were a child.

"But if you accept a fish as an animal you could argue that a carp does a lot of work," said Valerie.

"Define work," said Dave. Valerie waved him away without looking.

"But they don't work in a domestic or agricultural sector," said Sonja, still earnest.

"The carp is outside the capitalist system," said Katie from International Study Programmes.

"Since no monetary value is derived from his work, he is expendable," said Bob the professional translator. Bob was twenty years older and had bad hair and bad teeth and bad clothes; I sensed that Amanda might adopt him.

"Then I rest my case," said Valerie. "The carp is very Christlike."

"But we're not eating carp," said Sonja.

"If we were you could gaze into its mournful compassionate eyes," said Valerie.

"If we were, the carp would be dead," said Dave.

"Christ's love is eternal," said Valerie. "Obviously. Otherwise you wouldn't be here wishing him a happy birthday."

"Does your working carp walk on water?" said Amanda.

"When his throat is slit and his intestines jerked out, parts of him float a little bit," said Valerie.

"I have never understood," said Katie, "how vegetarians celebrate without something sacrificial in the middle of the table."

"You're right," said John, the international conference man. "That goes against all of Western history."

"Bread can be sacrificial," said Amanda. "Some people consider it to be human flesh."

"Fortunately this," said Katie, serving herself more Texas corn bread, "is not very convincing."

"I've never understood," said Dave, "how transubstantiation and defecation can be squared."

"Perhaps," said Sonja, "Martin Luther had this question, too."

"He was the first German to examine his stool," said Dave. "Searching for the presence of the divine."

Sonja scowled.

"Holy shit," said Valerie.

"More wine?" said Amanda. Everyone assented. There was something sacrificial in the way she split the bottle's throat with the blade of her corkscrew.

After dinner those of us who smoked took turns on the rickety balcony. Snow fell fast and thick, piling on the black grates and railings and the ground, turning the courtyard into a photo negative of itself. For a moment I thought that if I kept watching some vital clue would emerge and explain the death of our elderly neighbor. But it was cold and inside someone inevitably found *ABBA Gold* and pressed play.

Amanda was on the toilet four times before breakfast the next day while I hopped up and down on the other side of the door. Breakfast for each of us consisted of one sip of coffee and one spoonful of muesli. Then we took turns vomiting onto the splashy horizontal ledge of porcelain. Once our bodies had expunged all solids and liquids we each endured an hour of dry heaves. Both of us were trembling and sweating, wrapped in every available blanket, when we thought it might be safe to go back to bed and sleep it off. But my phone began to vibrate with all the Christmas guests reporting similar symptoms. We never identified the offending ingredient. We never had a dinner party again.

REVOLUTION

We began spending more—meals out, new clothing, and things for the flat. It was an era when things available elsewhere were becoming available in Prague, but with distinctly retro presentation. Fresh produce and lingerie both call for decent shop lighting. The department store nearest us, Kotva, was an enormous building that suggested a stealth bomber meeting a trash compactor. The interior layout was full of abrupt turns leading to surprising merchandise: teddy bears from Asian sweatshops in T-shirts that said *I'm love you*, Russian skis and skates and snowboards sporting inscrutable Cyrillic, American jeans at American prices.

Amanda had a talent for finding offbeat things—like an ankle-thick candle with an enormous painted wax scorpion climbing one side, a gaily painted life-sized wooden armadillo from Mexico, drinks coasters and place mats with stylized illustrations of bicycles and captions in twelve languages, wrought-iron bookends in the shape of grazing sheep, tea towel maps of obscure Scandinavian regions—so that Graceland quickly became a kind of personalized end point of globalization, as though all of history had led to us and only us living there. Some other tenant or tenants would have had less appealing champagne flutes and corkscrews.

Recycling at the time was for Czechs like some strange heathen ritual practiced in faraway lands. Instead a plastic crate lived behind the front door and when it was full of empty beer and wine bottles—every four or five days—I hauled it perspiring to the nearest shop (*lahůdky* or *potraviny*) and fed each bottle individually to a machine through a conveyer belt so that it could be rinsed, sterilized, and reused by whichever brewery or vineyard it belonged to. I thought it tiresome yet much more enlightened than creating whole recycling centers where everything gets smashed up and reconstituted. At times, hauling my individual burden of bottles around in the interest of the common good, I thought of recycling programs as exactly the kind of counterproductive capitalist hysteria that doomed capitalist ecosystems to begin with.

Amanda became very adept at inconveniencing me, with the usual things like blanket sharing and bathroom time allocation but more important with sets of unassailable priorities about which I had not been consulted: holiday plans and changes in the décor at Graceland. One Monday morning she seemed glum; in the afternoon after work I bought her some flowers. It was a favorite feature of Prague for me that every bus stop, tram stop, and Metro station had its own florist, so anybody off visiting anybody else could equip themselves conveniently.

I took her progressively more elaborate foliage through the rest of the week, culminating in a small olive tree. She never cheered up, and the tree lived and died on the balcony while she waited patiently for all the rest of the stuff to wilt. Later we had a gay cleaner once a week who ironed and folded my underwear while color-coordinating everything else. It may have been the nearest I saw Amanda to happy.

I also never understood how the British could take such a relaxed stance on coffee and timekeeping, among other things; Amanda could with evident ease greet the morning over a cup of mere tea and meet me somewhere a half an hour late with a smile. She smoked West Red, a Czech brand that caused me to retch, but refused to consider switching to a mutually agreeable brand, while pinching my Camels on the flimsiest of pretexts. She was always happy to relieve me of some portion of whichever variant of steak and potatoes I ordered when we were eating out, but she meanwhile cleaved to the dubious end of the shellfish spectrum. I once made the mistake of popping corn at home, and was prohibited from adding salt or butter.

Meanwhile she accused me of having a neurological condition that made me always do the wrong thing on purpose. If, for example, I said I'd be back at 10:30 Amanda knew nothing except the precise time I was guaranteed not to be back. If I promised to pick up some After Eights I was bound to return with a cheap Czech knockoff. When I promised tacos I made soup. None of these things was disastrous in isolation, she said. I pictured a secret notebook with all my transgressions logged by date, with illustrations.

She became distressed that The Relationship had become an independent entity and that she was often accused of leaving it out in the rain, or pinching its fingers in doorways; she felt when ordering coffee or withdrawing money from cash machines, that The Relationship was there, watching her, privately passing judgment on her choices and movements, and possibly filing reports for me on which areas of her conduct and deportment could use improvement. The Relationship was endlessly elastic, and assumed no definite form for more than a moment, and The Relationship was not gendered, yet not androgynous either, because it wore dark menswear and smoked Gauloises. If I went out and she listened to Louis Armstrong while folding laundry The Relationship wanted to know why she was not listening to Ella Fitzgerald instead. In her dreams The Relationship had a clown face and rode a bicycle while she trudged slowly uphill; on the far side she watched in horror as it zipped past her without brakes, but she always woke up before the crash. She felt that Graceland had a vulnerable third resident with unclear intentions.

I thought she was being silly. There was, I said, an ongoing stream of words between us, some shared experiences, and nothing else but an understanding that the arrangement should continue. She demanded to know why I couldn't come up with something a little more persuasive than that, and I said that if I mentioned love she might get mauled by The Relationship again. I asked why The Relationship couldn't just be a lovely sofa she could rest her lovely bottom on while reading about people less fortunate than she was or seeing them flick by on the evening news. I was happy to reupholster. She said, But what if there is a small fire under the sofa?

I thought The Relationship was a manifestation of the children we didn't have. We had discussed it several times. I thought that Louis or Linus could just live in a hammock slung between walls in the bedroom at Graceland for the first two or three years. Amanda countered that we might have a Louise instead, and naming a child Linus was probably abuse. Moreover where would all the stuff go? Was I volunteering to shift a pram up and down two flights of stairs daily, and if so, where did I plan to park it, the kitchen? I said that Louise was fine, or Lola or Lily or Lulubelle. I wasn't sure about the practicalities yet but I was sure that people in that part of the world had reproduced successfully for at least a couple of decades. Amanda suggested that I use my imagination on the matter of what a confined space might smell like once Larry or Lawrence or Lucy started on solids. I said that we could surely find a bigger place if she agreed on the main point of creating a small human together. She never said no but instead pointed out cruelly that first I would need a stable job.

THE ASTRONOMER'S NOSE

I am not sure when I noticed that Prague's favorite sons—native and adopted—all met grisly ends. Tycho Brahe's bladder burst and Mozart was probably annihilated by a contaminated pork chop. Kafka lost his voice first and his ability to eat second. Rilke succumbed to leukemia. The self-styled Mother of Cities is distinctly filicidal. No one is entirely sure what killed Dvořák at the age of sixty-two. I told Amanda perhaps we should move to Lausanne.

I became very interested in Brahe, who lost his nose in a duel, kept a dwarf as a jester and an elk as a pet until the elk died descending the manor stairs drunk—surprising, since the elk was accustomed to doing the same every night. Somehow despite the drink and drama Brahe accumulated forty years of astronomical observations that were more accurate and more meticulously gathered than any that were collected by anyone before him, using instruments of his own design incorporating metal instead of wood. In 1601 he died because, according to legend, he had to pee very badly but dared not interrupt his patron the emperor Rudolf II at one of Rudolf's Prague Castle banquets.

Modern testing of exhumed hair follicles suggested mercury poisoning, but further tests were needed.

I went one afternoon without Amanda to see his tomb in Prague's main cathedral. A flat marble slab bearing his name in capital letters lay in the floor beneath a vertical life-sized reddish-brown marble relief of him contemplating his own final resting place. He was, in my mind, the first scientist, although that honor is usually accorded to Galileo. I thought the sculptor had caught something, despite the armor, ostentatious mustache, and trappings of nobility; the expression on Brahe's marble face was that of a man bent on deciphering some new inscrutable evidence. I moved back to get a better look and stepped on a small child's toes.

No effort was made to hush the child, though there may have been a coordinated campaign to shame the transgressor, beginning with parental glares, spreading through surrounding bystanders. I apologized to the mother, and when that didn't work, the father, and when that failed, the child herself—a blonde girl of three or four, now swept into daddy's arms— who saw or heard me and buried her face in her daddy's chest, covered both ears, and howled in renewed protest. The vaulted ceiling, acoustically designed to make human voices mimic the chorus of heaven, failed to oblige. Without breaking her glare at me the child's mother tugged at the father's sleeve and they left before I knew what language the girl was bawling in.

"Quite a manipulative child," said a familiar voice in American English over my shoulder. I spun around to find Valerie laughing at me.

"She could have been a good Christian and offered me the other toes," I said.

"She gets what she wants," said Valerie.

"Where is Dave?" I said.

"He was an error," she said. I didn't press for elaboration.

"Where's Amanda?" she said.

"Busy," I said.

"Then you can help me with my implausible mission," she said.

"Which is what?"

"Investigating death. If Dave can write for *The Prague Post,* so can I."

I started tagging along with Valerie while she looked into, and wrote about, Brahe and Mozart, the phantom chimpanzee of Prague Zoo, the medieval monk who slew a prostitute in rage and himself in remorse on Celetná Street, where an outstanding Italian steakhouse now stands, and—at my suggestion—the nexus of floods, climate change, and carnivorous plants. Some of her work was published, occupying a full broadsheet opinion page with a commissioned cartoon. Kepler, she found, probably didn't murder Brahe for his data. Mozart, she found, almost certainly died from trichinosis. Subsequent generations of chimpanzees avoided an area of their enclosure where a newcomer was murdered by the alpha male thirty years previously because they didn't know that the alpha had been destroyed, and they were not spooked, wrote Valerie, merely waiting for the return of their once and future king.

Along the way Valerie told me or intimated that she came

from a screwed-up family in a bad neighborhood of a stupid town, and that growing up, she hadn't known whether she was going to be a hairdresser or a hairdresser. But she did write and publish original journalism without training.

"You're a self-made woman," I suggested one day over coffee in a riverside café.

"Everyone here is self-made," she said. "There is no system for making anybody. No corporate ladder or law school conveyor belt. That's what makes it all a colossal waste of time."

"Are you leaving?" I said, alarmed.

"Not yet. I have a stack of graduate school applications to fill out."

"Where and for what?"

"Monumental debt."

"You're dour," I said.

"I'm not complaining. I've enjoyed it, and it beats spinning pizza dough in Davenport. Realistically, do you want to go live with your parents again? That's where all this ends. I'd love to train as a scuba instructor in Thailand, but that's just postponing the inevitable."

"Let's distinguish between Davenport and living with your parents," I said.

"Davenport has a bridge I can throw myself off of," she said. "So does Prague."

COFFEE WITH MILK

I learned from my mother that back in the U.S. my aunt Donna was dying. Like Amanda's godfather she had some horrific lung disease, idiopathic pulmonary fibrosis, in which tissue slowly but inexorably decayed; she had maxed her oxygen tank out but just kept deteriorating. But she had, said Mom, an e-mail address now, and would surely like to hear from me.

Even before I got in touch, I had e-mails from other family members describing Donna as "difficult"; Aunt Carrie had visited Donna in Nashville and kept track of Donna's impossible demands on Uncle Joe with one eye on her watch. I pictured Donna on her deathbed, surrounded by treacherous siblings.

She died heroically, e-mailing me every few days until she couldn't anymore—about two weeks before her funeral, which she told me not to bother attending. When her father-in-law, my grandfather, died, I was twelve. She spotted me looking glum at his funeral reception, crossed the room, put an arm around me, and told me to get used to it. One of her last injunctions to me was to miss her a little, but not for long.

We didn't correspond much about her condition, aside from the panic attacks she had, despite the morphine, every time she levered herself off the portable toilet and back onto the sofa in the living room. I had slept on that sofa many times growing up. It was at least eight, maybe nine feet long.

We corresponded instead about me. The cost of living in Prague, she wrote, must be very attractive, but one day, perhaps soon, we'd want more space. Had I popped the question? *Get Amanda to tell me the colors in your apartment,* she wrote. *These things interest women, Elliott.* We must be having fine adventures in a place she could never have gone and could never go, she wrote. Make the most of it. But make plans, too.

She gossiped generously about the extended family, material that was particularly surreal to read in Prague. I had cousins I couldn't pick out of a perp walk, but I knew for a while which of them was getting a driver's license and who was off to Southern Methodist that fall. If there was one thing on God's green earth Donna couldn't see the point of it was a magnolia tree. For two weeks a year it just litters, and the rest of the time it blocks your view of the neighbors. She was lobbying my dad to chop his down. My mother, wrote Donna, seemed to have a new admirer in the shape of an Episcopalian priest. But she seemed to expect him to have God's own patience, too. Donna was pleased that once she was gone, Uncle Joe would have the sympathy and support of his sister Carrie. Donna told me she knew Joe was hers on the day he began taking milk in his coffee.

The sense of space and time and order implicit in her communication was utterly alien to a Prague dweller; nobody near Graceland had a garden, let alone a tree. Czech youth did not age; they went to sleep as children and woke up as adults sometime near the age of eleven or twelve. There were no priests. Taking Czech coffee black was unthinkable.

Donna sent, among other things, colorful Southern U.S. expressions for me to share with my students: "slicker than snot on a glass doorknob," "madder than a boiled owl," and my favorite, "I feel like I been et by a wolf and shit off a cliff."

My students appreciated the new phrases, though none of them could keep each one straight. Vlasta wanted to know more about the woman who supplied them. Since Uncle Joe was my mother's brother, Donna had married into the family, and therefore, said Vlasta, it was okay if I had a crush on her. Donna had decades of practice peering over her bifocals at entitled Nashville school brats to make a point; to this day anyone peering over glasses at me seems to be admonishing me. She was five foot one and built like an insect, with a middle Tennessee drawl that turned every utterance into a musical composition.

VIP

I went back to Indiana for two weeks without Amanda. Predictably on the first full day my mother scheduled a haircut and a dental appointment. During the rest of the week I also got a lot of new clothing and a string of lectures on alcohol consumption. I didn't smoke and I meant to stick to it. I saw my dad as little as possible—I found his midlife two-stroke Honda embarrassing, along with the chest hair spilling from rumpled linen shirts and the latest girlfriend whose high-heel-weary feet he rubbed obscenely in front of the television. She was or had been his postdoctoral student, thus I suppose a philosopher, too, which was no recommendation.

When my parents split up my mom spent a month on retreat at an archabbey in Indiana, one of only two in the U.S. and eleven in the world. He told his friends she'd gone to stay in a lesbian commune. She forgave him before I did.

Larry had cut my hair since I was old enough to climb into a barbershop chair, just as he had always cut my father's hair. His business partner, Jim, kept the books, I'm sure, but Larry in engineer boots and a perennial pompadour gave the barbershop its distinctive air. He chose the sports to display on TV, and I'm sure he arranged the stack of *Playboys* at the far end of the counter, which I was always shocked to see grown men looking at openly while waiting their turn. Larry ran the place as he might have run a Paris salon. In context that meant making jokes about Kentuckians and women, but he gave me jelly beans after every haircut until I graduated to Ski sodas, and when the price of a bottle of Ski jumped from 35 to 50 cents he took it like a man.

"So where you at?" he said, sweeping the apron around my neck.

"Czech Republic."

"Oh, Czechoslovakia," he said, correcting me. "You be careful. They got a lot of dictators over there."

"Not now," I said. "The president is a playwright."

"Now that's even worse," he said. "Imagine me running this country."

"We'd all have fabulous hair," I said.

"Thank you. That is true. Europeans might get quite jealous."

"Put the French right off their snails. Also, sports commentary would improve."

"Also true. I'd take executive action on that. You speak the language?"

"Not really," I said.

"My bank machine asked me the other day what language I speak," he said. "I do not like that at all."

"What do you tell it?"

"American is not an option. Is the food over there good?"

"Helps if you like cabbage."

"Women pretty?"

"Without exception. It's like wandering around in a wildly successful genetic experiment."

"Maybe it is," he said. "How come you don't have one with you?"

"I live with an Englishwoman who teaches English like me," I said.

"You went to Czechoslovakia to meet an Englishwoman? How come you didn't go to England for that?"

"They don't really need English teachers."

"Well, I'm going to make sure she likes your hair."

It occurred to me only after I left that he hadn't asked and I hadn't told him what sort of cut I wanted; by some ancient agreement I was always given one of the cuts appropriate for white Anglo-Saxon Protestant Hoosier hair. Shorn of my Bohemian identity I went to the dentist. I had been his patient for about ten years. I had chipped a molar in Prague months earlier, nothing painful, but it was best to get things like that seen to on my mother's nickel. My conversation with Dr. Sanders was necessarily short since there was Novocain involved. He didn't ask where I'd been.

"So what's it like," he said, "sitting around drinking wine all day in Europe?"

"Well, I work," I said.

"Uh-huh. Open up."

I complied, and remembered that having large fingers is one of the more advanced forms of rudeness available to a dentist.

"I see they have plenty of coffee in Europe," he said.

I tried to explain while he loaded a vicious needle that I lived in a beautiful city in a nice apartment with a charming woman and an adequate income.

"I guess everyone's got their problems," he said.

PART III

SMETANA

Amanda continued her upward drift in Prague society, teaching several officials at the Ministry of Finance and the Maltese ambassador to the Czech Republic. What the ambassador did all day was something of a mystery. At the embassy, however, she met an older couple—the first violinist of the national philharmonic and his wife, a cellist in the same orchestra. Prague's musicians earn their dinners playing embassies, she was told. She was invited to bring her American companion to lunch at their apartment on the following Saturday.

"You'll be invited to Prague Castle next," I said.

"Are you free?"

At the appointed hour we pressed a button next to a fourteenth-century gate and mounted a worn thirteenth-century staircase to a twelfth-century flat—all details relayed to us over lunch. Mrs. Radovan greeted us in a well-floured apron. She did not look tall enough to carry or play a cello. She was lean as a doe and her face, I sensed, was lined more by laughter than by worry. I judged her a youthful sixty. She led us into a living room with a fireplace, the mantle of which could have slept a family of five comfortably, also black from six centuries of soup preparation. It was not a large room—whatever palace it was part of had been ruthlessly partitioned into flats.

The living room where we sat was a matter of exposed brick and beam with timeless plaster between. A long sofa faced the fireplace with a veteran coffee table in the middle. Three mirrors of different sizes hung at different elevations above the sofa. At the end of the sofa stood a cabinet with a record player on top, and above the record player on the wall hung a violin and bow. There were two shabby upholstered chairs, one next to the door leading to the kitchen and the other adjacent to the fireplace. Mrs. Radovan explained that hundreds of years ago the bricks on the side of the fireplace were arranged in a curve to make sharpening knives while cooking convenient. Above the chair adjacent to the fireplace in a special alcove was the bust of Bedřich Smetana in black marble, looking very much like he had lost three daughters in infancy, his wife not long after, and his hearing at the zenith of his compositional mojo. The bust had at least been made before he lost his mind to syphilis. No fortune, success, or genius could compensate for such blows to the heart.

There was no dining room, just a dining table at one end of a large and surprisingly modern-looking kitchen in immaculate white with grey matte work surfaces and brushed steel handles and appliances. The bathroom was awkwardly accessed through the sole bedroom, where, I noticed, Mucha presided over the marital bed.

Mrs. Radovan implored us to sit. She spoke an unconfident English and called for her husband to appear.

Radovan walked with a cane even inside the flat, and his hand trembled visibly when he held it out to shake mine; it seemed to me that his fiddling days were numbered. Yet he was not much past sixty. He had the ear hair and nose hair and tempestuous eyebrows of an older man, and he somehow gave his cardigan the dignity of a waistcoat. He told me straight off the bat that he deplored American music.

"Dvořák wrote in 1893 that for American music to be great or distinctive or even American it must incorporate African American and Native American culture. And he put 'Swing Low Sweet Chariot' into the New World Symphony."

"So he predicted blues and jazz," I suggested.

"No," said Radovan. "He could not have foreseen the rise of the electric guitar, which is responsible for more pollution than anything but the automobile." He had the look of someone who could be quite savage about Kermit the Frog if provoked.

"When I must endure American garbage," he said, "which is anytime I leave my home, I try to listen for traces of gospel and sounds of joy."

He served us each a shot glass of Becherovka.

"All the potential that Dvořák heard was mutilated by the modern age," he said.

The beer Mrs. Radovan served in that household would have had Trappist monks volunteering for excommunication. The garlic soup was in appearance just croutons floating in hot water, but it lent Cartesian clarity to the mind and powerful curiosity in the gut about what was to follow. What followed was pork from Elysium and cabbage gathered on the slopes of Mount Olympus and bread dumplings kneaded on Paulina Porizkova's thighs. Radovan mentioned a pianist friend whose left hand drank more coffee than his right. Otherwise the conversation remained broadly derogatory.

The Radovans had one grown son, a mathematical wunderkind who had forsaken family and homeland to amass riches in Zürich; he had Westernized his name, discarded his accent, seldom wrote and never visited. I sensed furious disapproval from the father, but the mother spoke up hopefully for the boy's Swiss fiancée.

Radovan had no interest in visiting America because he like anyone else could taste the Great Plains just by listening to Dvořák. He had even less interest in visiting Britain, a place in his view historically plagued by musical illiteracy. Yet the more insulting he was the more cheerful he became (which struck me as rather British), and I could not really tell whether we were having a friendly conversation. Mrs. Radovan tried repeatedly to steer him toward more conventional topics like our favorite things to do in Prague, but he took her interventions as cues to hold forth still more. He talked for ten minutes about a culture and education minister in the early communist era who promoted Smetana (who had once lived in this very apartment, hence the bust over the fireplace) and disparaged Dvořák—and punished subordinates who strayed from his line. His point seemed to be that had we not been such ignorant young Westerners this elevation of Smetana over Dvořák would illustrate to us how profoundly perverse communism was. Alas, we could never grasp something so self-evident.

Mrs. Radovan asked where we would like to go that we had not yet been. Amanda mentioned the crypt on Resslova Street and both Czechs fell silent.

We had walked past the crypt several times and had seen the church walls peppered by thousands of rounds of machine-gun fire. We knew, roughly, that some Czech and Slovak paratroopers trained in Britain parachuted behind the lines at the end of May 1942 to assassinate Reinhard Heydrich, architect of the final solution and dread Butcher of Prague. We knew that the mission was barely successful, and that some days later the paratroopers, hiding in the crypt below Sts. Cyril and Methodius Cathedral on Resslova Street, were discovered and fought valiantly before committing suicide with the last of their ammunition.

"You must understand," said Radovan, "that for forty-one years every schoolteacher pronounced the assassins' names with dripping contempt. Then the Americans showed up and said you must build a museum to these great heroes. The British are especially excited about it. What Munich Agreement? Here is a tale of adventure and derring-do!"

He looked Amanda in the eye until she looked down.

"The Nazis had other monsters, of course. Things carried on exactly as they had, except for the thousands of Czech men, women, and children who were executed in reprisal. The entire operation was a stupid British publicity stunt."

"The men were brave," said Mrs. Radovan doubtfully.

"They were," said Radovan. "We built the museum. Selling fantasies to foreigners is what we do best. This is all ancient history, of course. Now you are free to send squadrons of young men here to decorate Czech cobblestones with English vomit every night on their stag party missions, so I have read, to find steak and tits."

I thought we were going to have to leave, or that I might have to challenge the old man to a duel for besmirching my lady's honor, or that perhaps sweet Mrs. Radovan had laced the dumplings with arsenic and we'd be under the floorboards by dusk with several centuries of other unwelcome guests. Yet Radovan's face was that of a man swearing he can't stand puppies, and he poured us more Becherovka.

"I'm afraid Dvořák just reminds me of sliced bread," said Amanda. "Old British TV adverts."

"What Munich Agreement?" cried Radovan. We all clinked.

SUICIDE

Two weeks later Amanda's parents came to visit from England. Mrs. Radovan kindly offered the flat to Amanda since the Radovans were going to be traveling at the time. Amanda's parents were thrilled to be staying not just centrally but at the pinnacle of continental high culture, the home of a great violinist and the former home of a great composer. They were also disappointed they would not get to meet the Radovans.

Every effort was made to ensure that I did not feel Amanda's parents were coming to inspect me. I had contributed a few words to some of her letters home, and I had spoken to each of them on the phone a few times, so it was not like meeting them cold. On the other hand, it was not like going to their house for a lovely home-cooked meal, either. They were coming to us for a week. Amanda said that my best behavior was just like all my other behavior. I replied that this was no reflection of how I felt on the inside. I might spend the next twenty Christmases with them and go bird-watching with them every spring. They were bound to think I was an idiot from the middle of nowhere, because I was. My prospective earning capacity could be measured in hellers. "That's true," said Amanda. "I'm not sure what I'm doing with you."

Amanda's mother was a sharply dressed, sharp-minded woman who muffled her opinions in irony; her father, a genial man with a fantastically reassuring voice. Yet I felt I hardly got to know them, or they me, because of sleep deprivation.

We greeted them at the airport and took a tram into town, then cheerfully cursed the wheels on their suitcases as we navigated cobbled medieval alleys. Amanda's parents were both retired from some obscure corner of the British film industry. When they weren't traveling somewhere they were busy planning to travel somewhere else. All of us were looking forward to the next five days.

Inside the flat the Radovans had left two sets of earplugs in plastic packaging with a note stating that things could get noisy in the city center at night. At just after 8:00 p.m. techno began thudding from a building across the narrow medieval street, and at 9:00 p.m. a forty-foot video projection of alternating strippers appeared on the opposite façade—strangely unappealing, because the various windows and windowsills meant that one woman appeared to have her head sewn back on six feet off-center, and another had her torso badly spliced down the middle.

Amanda discovered the heavy blackout blinds behind the curtains and drew them. The sounds of British stag parties trooping in and out and around began and intensified. We put on some of Radovan's Moravian folk music and sat around a table playing cribbage like a wholesome family unit living through some strange wartime occupation.

After her parents went home, Amanda announced that she was tired of living like a student.

"But you don't live like a student at all," I said. She was in the kitchen making paella, a phase she went through when she discovered that Kotva carried squid ink. "Look at the spice rack," I added. "We have turmeric and sage and bay leaves. I remember when we were just an oregano family."

"The spice rack itself is not very fulfilling," she said.

"It's probably not like having a child," I said. "But there's value in making a home."

"I'm not sure the spice rack is up to the job of making a home, either," she said.

"There's thyme. Cloves. Ground ginger. These are how you make the smells of home, at least."

"We have cayenne pepper, too. We can sneeze."

"If we got married we'd haul in loads of domestic presents," I said.

"We wouldn't have room for them," she said, the nearest she had come to taking marriage seriously. "We'd need a much bigger place to put them."

"Are you now aspiring to a mortgage?"

"No. You forgot to mention the saffron."

"We could always go live in Britain or America," I said.

"Oh, no," said Amanda. "Americans in Britain and Brits in America have the highest suicide rates in the world."

"Where did you hear this?"

"I read it somewhere. Each group thinks for years that they understand what is going on around them only to discover one day that they haven't understood a thing. Their marriages, jobs, and friendships all mean something entirely alien. You can no longer live in truth."

"Like if we woke up in Graceland but we were actually in Tennessee," I said.

"We're all fine in Japan, apparently. Crowded island with a rigid class system. But I can't help ascribing your accent a certain number of sincerity points," she said. "I could move to Indiana and discover that everyone is a complete wazzock. I'd have to move to Wisconsin."

"It's true that if I hear something in a British accent I have to repeat it in a Southern drawl to check if it really was smart."

"How do we know if we can understand each other right now?" she said.

One of her reforms was a smoking ban inside the flat. I stepped onto the balcony where we kept a studenty soup can filled with waterlogged cigarette ends. While I smoked I considered the fateful balcony across the courtyard. Fifty vertical feet did seem like a shallow, meaningless transition, an adjustment of coordinates. A horizontal shuffle of the same magnitude would do you no harm whatsoever. I had heard somewhere that to ensure success you should land on your chest. Perhaps he had done that, or perhaps he was just old and unlucky. I once locked myself into a girlfriend's apartment accidentally, and I had to jump from the balcony to get out. About eight feet. I bruised my heel badly.

Amanda joined me and wrinkled her nose as always at the courtyard stench of cabbage and urine. We pitched in with our sanctifying incense, moving our cigarettes to and from our mouths like censers, lustrating the air, to no avail.

MAZURKA

I spent a week proofreading a translated Ministry of Defense report on the effects of depleted uranium on plants, animals, and children. Of particular interest was the question of what happens when depleted uranium is introduced into the waterways of a desert ecosystem. Trees retreat, carcinogens climb ranks in food chains, and human birth defects and leukemia spike wherever the material is used. Millions of people will be tasting metal through their fingertips for generations to come, and inhaling radioactive dust. A conclusive study of these environmental and health effects, the report noted, would require the funding of a large, generous, and wealthy nation.

Amanda got both of us invited to an international symposium on "Politics and Morality" hosted by the Ministry of

Culture. The motto and starting point for all lectures and panel discussions scheduled was a line from Immanuel Kant: "Politics says be wise as serpents, with morality adding, as a limiting condition, and as guileless as doves." Participants included many eminent statesmen and intellectuals. Topics to be covered included "Politics and Faiths," "Morality and the Global Economic Order," and "Moral Europe." Economists flocked to Prague like alchemists did six centuries before them. Governors of places like Lower Saxony joined in, and the streets filled with famous academics. Wealthy Western wives clotted the quaint boutiques selling Bohemian crystal. Muslims with correct views were granted speaking engagements. Venues varied according to anticipated crowd size, but none of the events was held in Prague's hundreds of churches, eight synagogues, or lone mosque. That in itself said something about the era, said Amanda. Furthermore, she said, serpents aren't wise and Kant didn't give doves much credit.

All the speakers we saw were beautifully dressed. Several Scandinavians wore striking eyeglasses—colorful, bold, yet playful, and not garish. Every lecture hall had a population of handsome Germans with earnest faces, broad shoulders, and neckties in colors like iridescent salmon. Dapper and industrious Italians discussed GDPs in flawless English. Women, who represented about a third of the speakers across nationalities, did not bother looking businesslike—they wore flowers and birds and butterflies on blouses and skirts and scarves. British politicians looked tanned and relaxed and excited about juice bars. The Americans in particular moved with grace and ease and good humor, spoke knowledgeably about interest rates, and had the good manners to drink plenty of Czech beer and compliment their hosts on it. Amanda wore her poshest frock, a satin emerald thing over leather high-heeled sandals with thin straps around her ankles and calves. I had a velvety black jacket and some tapered coffee-colored French corduroys.

At the end of the convention we had dinner with the president of Poland and five hundred other distinguished souls. The Hotel Paris polished everything thrice beforehand, and drafted fifty blondes to deliver food and replenish drinks. The menu featured things like wild boar pâte, which didn't appeal to me; and pigeon breast with juniper berries; and salmon with grapefruit, which sounded more like art than food; and shelled spider crab with a creamy coral emulsion; and saddle of rabbit in Parma ham. Every table went through the agonies and intricacies of ordering rarified wines; I felt out of place when I ordered beer and rabbit. The Polish president, Nobel laureates, central bankers, and leftist firebrands all sat far away at the high end of the room, while we were at the table nearest the door.

If I could have confiscated the jackets, vests, shirts, ties, underwear, socks, shoes, handkerchiefs, cufflinks, belts, suspenders, wristwatches, eyeglasses, and wedding rings of the male guests, I could have bought a small house or two. Better yet I could build one: pillars of stacked shoes, laces entwined, could stand in each corner, while jackets with arms braided could hang between them as walls. The interwoven legs of trousers could serve as a roof. The lighter garments of the women could be hung as curtains or fashioned into soft beds. I had no plan for the newly naked guests.

After dinner and coffee several of the jackets and trousers

and wing-tipped shoes led the dresses and gowns to a large and almost empty adjacent chamber, where the cuffs arced like searchlights and the shoes scuffed each other while the gowns floated as if hung on balloons. A string ensemble played near the front of the room. We recognized the violinist from the blazing grace and dignity of his playing and the ineradicable grimace on his face.

During an interval Radovan, drenched in perspiration, spotted us and asked for a sip of my beer, a frank acknowledgment that he was very glad to see us. We admired his performance and asked what he had made of the whole conference.

He shrugged. "I'm sure it would go down very well in Vienna. What do you think?"

"Food's good," said Amanda.

"I have only a few minutes," said Radovan, handing me an empty glass. "Your parents," he said to Amanda, "left us a beautiful note offering us free run of their house at any time."

"Oh, good," said Amanda. "Will you take them up on it?"

"I have always wanted to hear the choir at Wells Cathedral," he said.

"I think the choir at Wells Cathedral would quite like to hear you," she said.

"I must return to my post. I'd be very pleased if you danced."

"I have no idea how," I said.

"We," said Amanda.

"With your permission," he said, slipping an arm around Amanda's waist, "I will show you. We are about to play a mazurka." He taught Amanda how to turn in half circles with occasional half hops.

The mighty waited.

Next he took me by the waist and the hand to show me how to lead. It consisted chiefly of counting to three repeatedly and pretending on every third beat that I had been shot in the thigh when I last led my troops into battle.

FLOOD

In late summer of our second year it rained biblically every day for over a week, and the river became very angry. By day three gulls appeared to be frolicking in fast currents, but by day five they looked terrified, and by day seven they and all of Prague's pigeons had fled for higher ground. It continued to storm, shower, and drizzle. The old dam south of the city was deemed adequate, dubious, and hopeless in short succession. Whole walls of water had to be released through the city. The river was increasingly thrilling to watch—we saw a waterborne railway boxcar racing toward Charles Bridge like a torpedo, diverted by an emergency crane. The boxcar couldn't be stopped or caught; the crane simply stuck a mechanical arm in the water and somehow survived impact without toppling and killing the operator. The boxcar slid under the bridge and took aim at the next one. Enormous uprooted trees followed suit. Soldiers lined the river's edge. Working flat out they got each sandbag placed moments before the water crested. Immense steel barriers lined riverside roads like toys put there for the river to play with. People gathered to watch the pulses released by the dam course through the city. The work of fifty soldiers over twenty-four hours vanished instantly.

I had a cell phone. Amanda didn't. I was walking to work on the eighth day of rain when Valerie called. We had been meeting for drinks after work while Amanda was busy or traveling, and we kept on top of each other's lives. She was close to hyperventilating, and it took me a moment to figure out that she had heard something about evacuations on Radio Free Europe. I told her to put a toothbrush and spare clothes in a bag and go to work anyway. I pointed out that even if evacuations were ordered there would have to be a notice period. Half an hour later while I was nursing a coffee and waiting for my computer to boot, Valerie called again, sounding suddenly like a field marshal and commanding me to return immediately to Graceland.

There was a notice taped to the front door of the building in Czech that even I could read. At ten o'clock the army was moving in and the residents were moving out. It was 9:48. I found Amanda upstairs hastily adding bananas and books to a stash of clothing. I was angry that she had not found a phone to call me; it felt like a minor betrayal in an hour of need. Yet there was no time to argue over it, and I made a mental note to thank Valerie later. At ten o'clock the army went from door to door as promised. A long line of buses awaited those without private arrangements. An ancient warning siren system was finally permitted to indicate that American bombers were inbound.

Amanda was barked at sharply in Czech. We boarded the nearest bus. If only there had been someone to bribe. Through the bus window we could see water bubbling up from sewer grates and manhole covers.

All but one of thirteen bridges were closed, and it took our bus two hours in creeping traffic to reach the school building that served as our shelter. We could only guess which part of Prague we were in because we could see Doom, defiantly beige against an aggressively dark sky. Inside the school gymnasium there were about two hundred cots and at least double that many people. We didn't try for a cot, just a patch of wall space to lean against. Most of the men sagely went to nearby pubs, and the hall was filled with stressed-out mothers berating their freaked-out children, but the dominant sound was that of helicopters thrumming outside in the rain.

I guarded our things while Amanda went to find a pay phone to call her parents. She returned an hour later and reported that the BBC was running nothing but flood, and we were just two of fifty thousand evacuees. She gave me directions to the phone and I called my mom. I imagined I could hear birds singing from her end of the line. I was staring through the tempered phone booth glass at the television tower. I burst into tears.

She said I should probably get back to Amanda and call again when it was all over. The CNN footage was shocking, she said. She was glad we were safe.

Over the next forty-eight hours, Amanda and I ate our bananas, slept sitting up with our backs against the gymnasium wall, and found a tolerable pizzeria within walking distance where we read our books. She ruined Kundera for me when she pointed out that his English translations omit Czech diacritical marks while retaining those of other languages, so Zürich has an umlaut over the *u* and Salvador Dalí gets to keep the smeary dotted *i* at the end of his name, but Žižkov is missing its butterflies.

Meanwhile in the city proper, nine people died, seventeen buildings collapsed, and hundreds of people became homeless, 280,000 public library books were ruined, and a gorilla drowned in a building that was submerged at the zoo.

Valerie was stranded at some other shelter in some other suburb, but from her we learned that some brave souls had begun breaking the quarantine once the waters began to recede, so we grabbed our things and set off, unable to find a road that ran straight until we came to the famous overland suicide bridge. The bridge was closed, but walking underneath it led us straight to the city center.

At the periphery of the devastation the only signs of life were automotive—ambulances, fire engines, and police cars. Farther in, soldiers limed the streets against disease. The air smelled of water and raw sewage and dead pets, and the sunshine was merciless. Outside our favorite cellar bars and restaurants stood heaps of tables and chairs and refrigerators and freezers covered in mud. The proprietors stood on the sidewalks openly weeping. They were permitted in, I think, to assess the damage. There must have been other residents sneaking in like us. The authorities had bigger things to worry about, and every soldier we saw looked pale and haggard and ready to collapse.

Both of us felt a burgeoning sense of shame. It had been exciting to watch the river rise, and the army spring into action, and to watch the mundane turn violent and new, to know that we were briefly at the center of the world's attention. It was commensurately horrific to examine in glorious sunlight the ruined livelihoods and wrecked aspirations of small business owners and young urban professionals and little old ladies who lived alone—every floating photo album, abandoned chair, smashed picture frame, and lost shoe implied a whole life carefully attended to and abruptly smashed for being in the wrong place at the wrong time. Yet both of us had inwardly cheered the flood on, because violence demands an audience. It was as though Prague were a person who had experienced some trauma, and she told us her story in incoherent fragments as we walked. Her sewers were breached, her streets violated, her foundations sabotaged, and although she could endure all that, her children were persecuted, too.

The evacuation notice still hung on the front door. We let ourselves in and stood listening for a moment in the foyer. We heard nothing. We climbed the two floors to Graceland, and I held my breath while Amanda put her key in the door. There was no damage aside from meat spoiled in the fridge when the power went. We still lacked power, but we had candles. Amanda made sliced avocado on crackers for dinner. We drank awful Moravian wine, a client gift we had been avoiding. She told me that if I were the last man on earth—which is how both of us felt in that place and that time—she wouldn't necessarily develop a space program. We went to bed early.

I don't know whether light or noise woke us up. A savage industrial rain pelted a megawatt moon. A malevolent angel hovered in the courtyard, bleating. Allied warcraft air-dropped demonic drummers on Prague. The body of Christ bled light from the punctures of a thousand machine-gun rounds. Gradually I realized there was a helicopter in our courtyard with a spotlight trained on our curtains.

We held hands under the duvet, not knowing if we were under attack, arrest, investigation, or suspicion. The courtyard echoed and amplified the whirling blades. The finger of light insisted.

Amanda suggested we wave, in case they were using thermal imaging equipment to check if we were alive and not stricken somehow. Both of us waved at people we couldn't see on the other side of the curtains. Almost immediately the helicopter left us first in total darkness and second in vast, marine silence.

REFLECTIONS

At the Golden Lion, Ivan announced that he had been offered a job—headhunted, in fact—by a conglomerate vast and diversified beyond description. His job would entail evaluating culpability in catastrophic events around the world. He was moving to London, although—Ivan hoped—only for long enough to make an obscene pile of cash. The catastrophic events were predicted to pick up speed anyway, thanks to climate change, resource depletion, and postmodern logic in political circles.

"It's a strange arrangement," said Ivan. "Because Britain doesn't actually make anything. All they make is Excel spreadsheets. When I went for interview I didn't see a single employee enjoying a cigarette. The business is completely divorced from the business. So I don't know. I'm moving from a regional post of tangible realities to an international post that feels to me largely theoretical. I might gradually cease to exist."

As a sort of farewell, Amanda and I were invited to spend a weekend at Ivan's country cottage—his dacha. Otherwise we might never have learned that he had a wife and two kids. The dacha was essentially a camping cabin with an enormous cellar under a trapdoor for storing beer. Mrs. Ivan—Rosa—emerged from a bedroom periodically to prepare meals. The boys, Milan, nine, and Jarek, seven, climbed trees and waded in streams and threw rocks at each other while Ivan sat in a lawn chair in the sun with beer. The countryside began at the door. "What am I going to do with them in the city?" he said with a sweep of his hand. I could see from what he said and the cold weight of the beer in my hand as I sat in my own lawn chair that I was experiencing one of the higher forms of civilization. Occasionally he had to shout but never move. The cell phone his employer had issued him received no signal within ten minutes' walk. In the mornings he chopped wood or played tennis.

Inevitably I thought of Milan's dead twin, of a life that should have been lived: trees climbed and apples picked and knees skinned; humiliation and emasculation time and again at the whims of lovely young ladies; groveling and degrading himself for fifty years just to pay rent; and ultimately passing the whole arrangement along to some miniature half clone and showing him or her how it is all done. And I thought of Milan's compulsive tennis playing, as if he could never get enough because he was always playing for two. He had gone recently on a tennis holiday in Spain—a mistake, he told me. The other guests had seemed more interested in who was playing on the next court over than in the game itself, and he had developed a special disdain for what he called "social tennis."

Amanda got quickly bored. An hour or two of beery babysitting was her outer limit. She took a couple of walks on her own but felt stared at like the village eccentric—like if she had a dog she might have had an excuse, she said. Privately she told me that she couldn't figure out what the hell Rosa did all day. After the boys were asleep Rosa came outside to sit by the fire and sip something stronger than beer, but for the longest time she would not be drawn out in conversation.

While Ivan and I drank to his hard work and good fortune again and again and again, Rosa finally opened up to Amanda. There was in Rosa's mind an idée fixe called Western Woman, and Amanda realized Rosa was trying valiantly to become one overnight. In the first place this meant improving her English, and in the second place it meant absolutely everything else. What to wear, how Amanda got her exercise, how to cook food that had failed to evolve or improve since the Second World War, how to avoid roving packs of vicious football hooligans, and what time to serve tea to the neighbor ladies—all came up for discussion, along with how to dress the boys.

"Well, we don't really do high tea anymore," said Amanda.

Ivan was chiefly aghast at the prospect of room temperature beer.

I had a momentary recollection of my first aspirations with Amanda—venturing into terra incognita together, our world a stable arrangement of pillows and coffee and books, with events and other people elsewhere as chaotic as they liked to be; how I had planned to borrow my opinions on movies and politics from her to spare myself the trouble of thinking.

Rosa was turning herself into a new woman, Ivan into a new man. Amanda and I were both bored at age twenty-six. Moreover the boredom itself seemed like some form of heresy for the two of us, sworn enemies of boring things like mortgages and careers. Ivan and Rosa were our reverse image, westward bound, with diametrically opposed intentions.

COLD WAR

Amanda made several trips on her own. A Russian oligarch's wife was buying Russian *Vogue,* so she flew Amanda to Monaco for a week of immersive English-language training around the racetrack and the roulette wheel. The Latvian central bank engaged her for intercultural training. I was proud of her. I hadn't imagined that teaching English as a foreign language could be a whole art form and lifestyle all at once. I used to watch her hips as she walked through the airport departure gates, an insouciant roll, a suppressed swagger, and a promise that when she returned she would still be mine. A nuclear power plant under construction in Tajikistan required its engineers to learn to communicate with their Western overlords. She phoned me from Dushanbe; I heard a thin click on the line. I am sure we were both put under surveillance. She told me that the British consul arrived at the airport twenty minutes after she landed at 3:00 a.m. She had some visa trouble but he seemed to have known she was coming. The connecting flight from Moscow had been full of itinerant fruit pickers. She managed to communicate with them using rudimentary Czech. Changing rubles at Domodedovo was a special form of hell. In Dushanbe she was shadowed everywhere. It was impossible, she said, to distinguish between secret police and pervy men.

In her absence I migrated among various pubs. At work Hana and I churned out an endless succession of translations of Czech News Agency bulletins for the *Prague Business Journal* and *The Prague Post*—in a sense I was responsible for more *Post* copy than Dave was. The gist of it all was that wherever you looked, somebody's money was missing. Apparently some people in New York and London found this distressing. After work I detected a citywide influx of fine ashtrays, fine barstools, vibrant wallpapers, intriguing contemporary art, excellent sound systems, and gleaming brass bar fittings. At last Czech beer had the accoutrements it deserved. Peering into the details was just churlish.

I met some strange people. One Englishman in a Žižkov bar insisted that he made a living smuggling penguins. He claimed to service a niche of an international black market between zoos. I pressed him on the obvious questions of storage and transportation of merchandise. He had a ready answer about refrigerated shipping containers and frozen warehouses in the deep countryside. I asked how he fed the penguins. "Things are like gulls," he said. "They'll eat anything." He was vague about price per beak, since it depended heavily on what a client zoo could pay—Tokyo and Nairobi played in very different leagues. I thought at the time that he was merely a mischievous drunk;

only on the following day did it occur to me that I might have been speaking to James Bond.

The following night I met three very friendly Russians named Dasha, Masha, and Pasha. They claimed they had got lost looking for Mexico. When I asked how long they were staying Dasha said maybe lunch or maybe dinner. In retrospect I felt sure they were checking me out.

My paternal grandfather worked for the CIA. Amanda's first cousin Paul was shot dead by an IRA sniper on his first day patrolling South Armagh at the age of nineteen. I couldn't imagine that either of us fit any profile of people who like to run around damaging national interests. Amanda suggested when she returned that the new definition of *dissident* was someone who dares to leave home.

In the '70s both superpowers were competing to industrialize sub-Saharan Africa. My grandfather supervised various new factories in Nigeria and Kenya. The only thing he ever said about his other, covert work was a casual aside to my dad: he copied the serial numbers from heavy machines, and so did his Soviet counterparts. He knew and they knew and he knew that they knew and they knew that he knew, so they all enjoyed sipping coffee together in the mornings and discussing the weather. One afternoon in Nairobi his car exploded while he was in a shop with his servant. The bomb, however, was intended for a visiting diplomat who also drove a blue Peugeot. At least, that is what he told the family. My grandmother knew nothing of his CIA involvement until after his death, when the government sent her a letter commending his dedication.

In a more civilized era, Amanda could have been a valuable, coffee-slurping, sunshine-evaluating asset. Instead she was rudely called to the British Embassy in Prague and told to be careful about going to sensitive places on a freelance basis. If she could show documentation of institutional backing, red flags might not be raised by the apparently guileless and objective system. Amanda replied that she was going to spend a week of the following month teaching at a Swedish paper mill.

I lounged around with takeaway burgers and fries whenever she was away; she said she wished I traveled more so she could know what that was like.

Valerie asked if I would like to join her in a visit to Benátky, the modest manor house outside Prague where Tycho Brahe had lived, if only to see the steps the elk rolled down. I agreed. Valerie and I caught a local train, a smoke-filled two-carriage thing useful for outrunning glaciers, and from the station where we disembarked it was a two-mile walk on gravel roads to reach the house. "No wonder," said Valerie, "nobody has written about this place before." A tree-lined drive became an exclamation mark at an unused circular fountain in front of the house, as if the whole thing were designed for vintage sports cars to turn around in front of. There were no cars or signs of other visitors, but the front door, an enormous mélange of wood and iron, was ajar. On the other side of it a plastic bucket with a lid sat on a desk next to a pentalingual sign soliciting donations. There was a chair next to the desk, suggesting that someone was around somewhere, but enforcing the donations policy clearly offered that person ample opportunity for refreshment elsewhere. Valerie slipped a fifty-crown note in, which was worth at least two beers.

A staircase in soft worn white marble addressed us fifteen feet from the door, broad, gentle, and incompatible with visions of rolling elk. In a gallery through a door left of the staircase Valerie found a leaflet explaining that the manor had been inhabited until 1948. To the right of the staircase I found a small but beautiful library. One shelf was devoted to recent spy thrillers in French.

Upstairs we found several bedrooms and another set of stairs too narrow for antlers, leading, according to a sign on the wall, to Tycho's observatory.

The sign was misleading; the floor above contained a cramped room full of curious objects like toys. Arcs and angles, rods and spheres of bronze pointed and pivoted and spoke mutely of math; small cards identified each item as a sextant, quadrant, or armillary sphere and informed us that each of them established in theory what the eyeball could establish in practice only through a telescope, which had not been invented when Brahe lived. Each item was a miniature model of some final law of the universe, and together they illustrated the ultimate economy of things; motion was meaning. The concentric mobile circles of an armillary sphere represented God's onion, and the pie-slice wedge of a sextant was an aperture leading to an all-encompassing view. The originals had all been destroyed in the Thirty Years' War; we were looking at reconstructions drawn from Brahe's copious writing and drawing. An artist's note underscored Brahe's optimism—a conviction evident in every component of every instrument that someday all speculation and superstition would be swept away by the universally intelligible language of measurement. Photocopies of Brahe's colorful illustrations hung in some cases above or next to the re-created instruments.

"With funding this place could really be somebody," said Valerie.

I lingered longest over a mural on the south wall. If, I read, there had been no ceiling, and it had been nighttime, and I had been somewhere in Brahe's native Denmark, I could have charted the passage of stars overhead to within two arc minutes by referring to the mural. I didn't know what an arc minute was or how such a thing might have worked. On the wall a pitiless maiden withered a lovelorn swain with a glance discarded over her shoulder, a goat eluded a yeoman while his lord tipped a wineskin, a boy tugged a rope attached to a bell much bigger than he, and a knight struggled to restrain his innards erupting from a mortal wound. None of these things corresponded to any constellation I knew of—some interpretive key was missing. The original mural, I read, was painted by Brahe himself, who also left behind a great legacy of poems in Latin. Death quells many things, read the artist's note, but not communication. Anyone could see that five hundred years ago there was still some reason to hope.

There was also a small exhibit dedicated to the astronomer's nose. A drunken student brawl, clashing steel, one fateful swipe through the upper cartilage. Both duelists retired, honor presumably satisfied. Whether Brahe's prosthetic bridge was silver, gold, copper, or bronze remained a mystery. A fashionable man, he may have alternated noses between home and state or court occasions. Perhaps he had one nose for science and another for love. Perhaps the love nose had an elaborate case and a variety of polishing rituals unknown to all but its wearer. It was horrible to consider Brahe's nose falling out in the middle of seducing some local wench: all that intelligence, prestige, wealth, and power instantly ridiculous. Better to hide forever, publishing nothing in the cold companionship of stars, leave the question of celestial immutability to somebody less deformed.

Worse still, after all he had accomplished and bequeathed to humanity, he was remembered chiefly for his nose.

TUMBLEWEED

Amanda wrote from Berlin, where she was teaching for two weeks. Germans, she grumbled, were far too progressive in making youth comfortable around obsolete technology. The public library where she planned her lessons was loud with chatter and chirping phones and elaborate mating rituals between students, all of them equipped with soft drinks and laptops. But construction work outside her hotel room window commenced at 8:00 a.m. sharp, so she couldn't work there.

Valerie invited me for a drink at La Casa Blŭ, a sleepy saloon by day and a crucible of excess and abandonment by night. We met at 6:00 p.m.

I had become tired—perhaps under Amanda's influence—of Americans with their wrenching personal problems, which all seemed to call for the same gravity as the death of a parent or the illness of a child; perhaps it was just the Americans that we knew in Prague, but it always seemed to require a half hour or forty-five minutes' interrogation to determine that really the person in question was just bored or frustrated, or, perhaps, mildly depressed. I hoped that Valerie and I could just drink and not swap life stories.

The coat she wore was stoplight red and she seemed to illuminate the room. We talked about new restaurants and new shops (we could eat at the Brazilian place later if I liked). She told me that after her parents divorced she had grown up in a neighborhood she described as a refuge for formerly wealthy people. All the children played together outside and all the parents were friends; it was like Mexico without the disease, poverty, crime, corruption, and sunshine. Before the divorce they had lived in a neighborhood with plenty of money and plenty of children, but the children didn't really play together and neither did the grown-ups. Her mother had remarried, and Valerie had a couple of stepsisters. But more important her father had figured himself out, and he was always happy to hear a soccer ball smack against the living room window—as proof that all the formerly wealthy people were raising happy, healthy children. The most tragic thing that had ever happened to her was that she wanted to pursue ballet, but when she got to college she realized that she was a head taller than everyone else, and a professor suggested something modern instead.

Two or three drinks in I found myself describing my own wrenching personal problems; I had always imagined myself with tenure and three children like my father before me, but unlike him I was going to make my marriage work. I couldn't get started, though, because somewhere in there Amanda had spotted a job description she didn't care for, and my aunt's death shadowed everything like a cloud riveted permanently into the sky. I couldn't see the point of remaining in Prague and I would never return to Indiana, and I was increasingly unemployable in both places anyway.

Valerie had a liberating way of not caring about anything I told her; she was patient with my navel-gazing but there were more important things to do, like drink and be merry.

I considered being annoyed but she had moved on to another frivolous and inconsequential anecdote: how her father's colleagues in the 1980s before the divorce had joked that he needed a wife, and he had said everyone needs a wife; my wife needs a wife. I said again that I felt sort of blighted by my own decision to flee from reality and live in Bohemia, and she told me the uses of castor oil in torture and childbirth. I gave up and followed in her unpredictable wake, and I began to enjoy it. Later when she suggested dancing it seemed like a good idea, and still later when she kissed me it seemed like a mistake that I could easily overlook the next morning.

For the rest of that week I oscillated between feeling very alive and feeling very unworthy of that distinction. It was a week of deeply anguished conversation with our clothes off. Valerie had neglected to mention that she was not remotely cheerful at home, and that in addition to her profound relationship with her body she also had a bellicose arrangement with her self-esteem; for my part I learned that although I came across as confident and self-assured at first, I was clearly misrepresenting myself; moreover she didn't like scrambled eggs and found my indecisiveness about what else we might have for breakfast supremely irritating. Both of us were disappointed with our compromise of butter on toast, if only because the bread was that horrid Czech stuff with cumin seeds in it, and she was going to lose her patience if I talked about Amanda anymore . . . Some of my deficiencies that came to light that week included a slow speech pattern; listening to every remark was like watching a tumbleweed roll over the Indiana desert, she said; and she noted my stupid expression, whenever the prospect of more sex arose, as though I thought I was about to go on an excursion. I managed to get through most of her wine.

LAUNDRY LINES

"It is a shame," Amanda had said, "that we never married. I think divorce is rather glamorous, like getting out of rehab."

She was aggressively cheerful during her last week in Prague, when she slept in the bedroom and I slept on the kitchen floor. She had taken a day or two to absorb things, privately. Once her mind was made up, however, her feelings were clearly none of my business. She practically chirped *good morning* and *good night* as a form of punishment. When I asked what she was going to do back in Britain, she said she might train to be a librarian. I couldn't tell if she was serious. Initially she'd have to work in a nursing home or a call center flogging conservatory windows. She made that sound like a thrilling adventure. She spent every evening that week out for farewell dinners and drinks—she was immensely popular—but she said she didn't tell anyone what had happened. I suspected she kept quiet for her benefit, not mine. I wanted to stay in touch. She agreed to that unconvincingly. I noticed when she packed that she didn't pack anything associated with me. She said one morning that she was looking forward to boring people with her story of how she once had dinner with the president of Poland.

I tried endlessly to put myself inside her head imaginatively if only to see what damage I had done. Not how she felt about my betrayal per se but what pictures of the future I had shattered and what aspirations I had compromised. What devastated me most on reflection was the idea that I would never see our child strapped across her chest like a grumpy albatross. I'm sure this thought did not trouble her. But it was precisely because we did not have plans, children, assets, mortgages, or even careers that what I had done was so terrible. All we had had was each other. When I had tried to explain this she had reassured me that I'd done us both a favor.

Afterward I was living off beer purchased with loans from my mom that I had no realistic plans to repay. At work Hana had requested a reassignment because my increasing distraction imperiled her ability to pay rent; soon afterward Terence fired me. I couldn't have paid the rent for Graceland solo, anyway—though I did, for a few months, at Mom's expense, spend mornings and afternoons on the sofa with coffee and books or newspapers, a parody of domestic contentment. And yet a little earlier each day I took my empty bottles to the *lahůdky* and exchanged them for eight full bottles of Radegast so I could marinate in sorrow on the courtyard balcony while the evening grew dark and cold. I felt, at last and at least, kind of Czech. I knew that I was supposed to cheer up and look for a job, but I also knew the natural order of things. Women hung out the laundry on lines. Later they reeled it in again. A man's white linen long-sleeved shirt, still wet, spiraling oddly as it fell, was the nearest thing to meaning or beauty there was, but that meant the woman had to go down there and fetch it and wash it again.

I couldn't be bothered to clean the flat. The garbage can was overflowing with the greaseproof paper that came with cheap Polish sausages on Wenceslas Square, the bedroom floor was a Sierra Madre del Sur of dirty laundry, and the kitchen sink looked like the Somme in 1917. The bathroom had developed an overall slime shield to defend itself against whatever I had planned.

If not reading or drinking, I was taking long walks around Prague. I could read if not understand most shop signs I saw, like "Fresh Pet Meat Daily," and I could identify the languages I overheard, even distinguishing between Czech, Polish, and Russian. I could, if necessary, talk vaguely about hockey in a bar, expressing support for one goalkeeper or team or nation over the other. Yet I somehow didn't see Prague anymore in my walks, most of the time, only my shoes hitting the pavement or the kitten heads again and again and again. I was sometimes aware of crossing a highway overpass or a river bridge and I sometimes noticed the rain. Often I crossed the famous suicide bridge at Nusle—the communists, Ivan had told me, never installed safety measures, because they respected your decision. To avoid total self-absorption I once or twice fed the ducks at the millrace on an island in the river under the castle hill.

I had to look up at times, though. Prague was designed to confuse medieval invaders—and without Amanda to consult it was all but impossible to reach a given destination even if it could be seen all the while. Turn left, turn right, and go straight were all meaningless, and usually prohibited by signage; drift, amble, and meander were the only means of getting anywhere, which proved on arrival to be more of an elsewhere anyway.

WHEN YOU NEED HELP

I called Mr. Cimarron at last in despair. He asked me if over the following weekend I would like to search for Stalin's bottom. When I asked what he was talking about he asked if I owned a flashlight. I said I'd prefer not to examine Stalin's bottom if that was what he was proposing. That was no longer possible, he said. I said that I could probably purchase the required item if he would please enlighten me in the meantime. I had told him what had happened, and I think his main purpose was to distract me.

The largest Stalin monument ever erected, he told me, had stood in Prague on the banks of the Vltava looking over the water toward the Jewish Quarter and the rest of the city beyond. Made of granite, fifty-one feet tall, and seventy-two feet in length, because several workers and soldiers stood behind Uncle Joe, like a full-bodied Mount Rushmore with regular people instead of corrupt oligarchs, and not built on land confiscated from indigenous people whose ancestors immigrated from Siberia twenty-five thousand years ago. Even Stalin's jacket button was one meter wide. Mr. Cimarron said that granite was used only on the exterior, with reinforced concrete inside, so the whole thing was a kind of cream-filled chocolate bunny for a rock-eating monster at Easter time. The structure was demolished with eighteen hundred pounds of dynamite in 1962, when Stalin worship had gone out of style.

The interesting thing, he continued, was the space beneath it, originally designed to become a mausoleum for some Czech hero sufficiently worthy to spend eternity in a glass coffin beneath Stalin's boot. It had instead been used to store potatoes for several years. After the explosion, the mausoleum had become a kind of demolition dustbin where Stalin's ears and eyebrows might have fallen, and a truly intrepid and crafty explorer might uncover the ultimate trophy, a piece of ass.

I pointed out that decades had elapsed, and that, moreover, eighteen hundred pounds of dynamite sounded awfully thorough to me.

"Ah, but the flood," he said. "Everything must have been rearranged in there. It will be like panning for gold."

"Surely," I said. "Stone Stalin was fully dressed. We're not going to find any telltale anatomical signs."

"Yet the talismanic power of the thing beckons me from here."

"I won't need a flashlight because it will glow," I said.

"Exactement."

I bought a flashlight from Kotva as we walked to the site. Mr. Cimarron provided further background.

"The man who designed the Stalin monument committed suicide with sleeping pills on the day before the unveiling," he said. "It is not known why. He had previously designed monuments to a religious reformer and the first president of the republic. Those were destroyed by the Nazis."

"He lived at the wrong time," I suggested.

"Everyone does. It would require extraordinary moral flexibility to honor both Masaryk and Stalin in the same lifetime. I think he concluded that he didn't have it. And yet the rest of the population did."

"Does," I said.

"The designer was one of seven deaths associated with the monument. One fellow opened his skull on Stalin's knuckle by falling drunk from some scaffolding. Later another took a smoke break next to some dynamite. It's all a bit like one of your American cartoons."

"Can you imagine," I said, "the amount of dust resulting from the marriage of that much granite and that much explosive?"

"Which is why when we find the sacred stone, we must both kiss it." He was silent for a moment, eyeing me. "I find it usually best, by the way, not to confess. If caught, never apologize. Simply say I am who I am."

"That sounds like a negotiating position," I said. "But we are talking about love, not money."

"One day perhaps you will grow up."

I had made a point of walking past Mr. Cimarron's shuttered Žižkov studio every few months, and if he was there, asking him out for a beer. On a previous visit the studio was empty except for some trash bags, a broom, and the artist, who said he was giving up. I fetched a brace of beers from a nearby corner shop and returned to hear why.

"I'm tired of making comments," he had explained. "I try to make objects. I specifically try to make objects that don't and can't comment. It is impossible. Even if I wanted to comment on things," he added, "commentary itself has just gone postmodern."

"The appropriate comment is silence," I suggested.

"Ganz genau."

"What are you going to do instead?"

"I don't know. Talk to small children and remember their names."

"These children will pay your rent?"

"I like metalwork. Jewelry does not comment very loudly. I will sell trinkets to tourists on Charles Bridge."

"They're not going to pay you six thousand dollars per item," I said.

"As a novelty act I will make jewelry blindfolded while they watch," he said.

"They're still not going to pay you six thousand dollars."

"Money does not exist," he said. "Only debt exists. Morally, financially, historically, and otherwise. It's the economy from which all other economies hang."

"I have no idea what that means," I said. "It sounds like you are dropping out of the economy."

"Better than dropping out of the sky."

"Do you have a girlfriend?" I said. "Who lets you out of the house in this frame of mind?"

"I have some entanglements."

"Sounds dreadful."

"Traditional. In that and other respects I don't belong in this century."

"Nobody does."

"You don't belong in this century either, but otherwise you are wrong. Nihilists do."

"These entanglements of yours. Are they supportive? Do you talk about this stuff?"

"They are all rich."

"Is that a yes or a no?"

"I will continue to eat, bathe, sleep, and drink beer."

"You're not dropping out of the economy. You're just becoming a prostitute."

"Debt is a bitch," he said.

"Can you please just write some of this stuff down somewhere? For your own benefit if for no one else's."

"That would be commenting."

"You are commenting right now," I said.

"Nothing said over beer really matters," he had said. "Only that something was said."

As we approached the failed mausoleum, Mr. Cimarron said it was colloquially called the Grotto, and described it as an integral fixture of his adolescence. It had been for a while a popular trysting place, but portable cassette players ended that: it became a place for building fires and listening to banned Western music, with a sentry to launch a rock into the water if the authorities looked likely to take an interest. Concrete columns, iron joists, and shattered stone became layered in graffiti; the Grotto was an alfresco nightclub with décor that changed every week. Chain-link fences had surrounded the area but holes were cut and trees climbed. Since the revolution the Grotto had been covered and almost sealed by a plaza popular with skateboarders, and at one point an eleven-foot inflatable Michael Jackson had held court there for a month. Veterans such as Mr. Cimarron knew, however, of an airshaft and a wall fissure hidden in trees, and what's more, he said, I was perfectly cast to play Indiana Jones. The gleeful violence of the river must have stirred the soup of stone and mud inside the Grotto, desperate to erase all memory of anything that had ever happened there.

The river was dappled and placid as we crossed over a bridge; despite the cold there were even young men rowing young women around on rented boats. Frequently they had to dodge the immense barges crowded with tourists who gossiped and drank beer, while a guide recited boring historical anecdotes into a crappy loudspeaker. At the far end of the bridge we crossed a busy ancient road with tram lines slashed into the cobblestones and came to the wide staircase leading to the top of Stalin's plinth. Mr. Cimarron led me to the right side of the staircase and onto a small trail through the adjacent woods, past Coke cans and beer bottles and filthy sleeping bags on flattened cardboard boxes. The wall alongside us was slathered in graffiti consisting mostly of profanity in English. We reached a rusting iron door mostly shut but bashed ajar enough to squeeze through with determination. Mr. Cimarron switched on his flashlight and slipped lithely through. I struggled and grunted after him.

A short rubble-strewn corridor decorated in used condoms led to a rectangular chamber of about the same dimensions as my high school gym. There was a foul stench of human sewage, rotting vegetation, and fetid/putrid water, but at least it was warm inside. Mr. Cimarron's flashlight beam moved slowly, methodically, assessing the chunks of rebar, spikes of iron, tree trunks, fire pits, trash heaps, orphaned shoes, vinyl record fragments, vodka bottles, pizza boxes, terra-cotta tiles, clothespins, corrugated tin panels, broken ladders, calendars, dishwashing liquid bottles, wooden planks, aluminum cans, red bricks, plastic guttering, chicken wire, ballpoint pens, dirty magazines, frying pans, lead pipes, postcards, coffee mugs, and other detritus it found. I was sure Mr. Cimarron would consider it some fascinating sort of art, but I felt that we had discovered instead a monstrous and desolate womb.

MOM

It was entirely humiliating when my mother came to Prague to get me. She pretended she was making an oft-promised visit, but she also asked in advance when my lease ran out and what my prospects were, so I knew before she arrived that she planned to persuade me to come home.

We did some sightseeing, but what impressed her most was the way the Czechs seemed very respectful, like Americans of the 1950s, she said, an observation and a comparison that no one else would make. She took endless photos of stained-glass windows, and I pitied the friends who might one day endure them. I frequently lost her in crowds, a little Indiana hen among enormous Czech chickens, but she had a knack for finding me.

She said she was sad never to have met Amanda, but reassured me that someone else would come along. I pointed out that somebody else had come along, and that was the problem. Mom, sounding very like Amanda, said that I was still young.

She had a list of people to buy gifts for, so we trawled the open-air markets examining wooden chess sets, Bohemian crystal, Russian dolls. I made sure that she was very careful with her handbag.

She was somehow less maternal, as if it was time to accept that I screwed up sometimes, and she made jokes she wouldn't have made to me before ("The first time your child says 'Mama' is priceless. The 100,000th time is torture"), and above all, she seemed genuinely interested in Prague, not preoccupied with her mission. We took long leisurely strolls, which delighted her at every turn, passing a Carpathian church in the woods under Prague Castle, seemingly assembled from gingerbread matchsticks and transported intact from Ukraine half a century previously. Above the entrance gate of the Slovenian embassy we found a man-sized marble vulture just waiting for someone to die in the street.

I took her to the Golden Lion, which was an emotional mistake for me, because the décor had been Westernized. A wagon wheel chandelier hung from the ceiling and rusty farming implements dangled from the walls. An upright piano darkened one corner, and rag dolls and miniature barrels and willow bouquets lay arrayed artfully in baskets where there were lees and eddies in food and drink traffic, with a kind of ambience that said, *Relax, you're not in Europe anymore.* I found myself appalled by innocence again.

"You may find it difficult going home," she said, after we had both ordered pasta. "Like a terrible English lesson in your head. Looking around at Americans and saying, *Why do these people do this? Why did they do that? What the hell are they doing now?*"

She asked if I was still thinking of graduate school, but I told her I had gone off history altogether.

"She sounds to me," said Mom, changing subjects abruptly, "a tad selfish. You have not had an easy time."

"I haven't?"

"And you helped her with her work."

I could not imagine my mother approving of Mr. Cimarron, or for that matter Milan, and the way he usually sat glowering without saying much. She insisted on meeting everyone, though, so we convened along with Vlasta around a table in a beer garden on the sort of day when the sun renders the architecture completely irrelevant. I quietly hoped that my former students would not practice any of their American slang. We had an hour of awkwardly swirling small talk. Only afterward did I grasp that my mother had been gathering witness testimony in the investigation of a crime.

"You had sympathy," she said, "everywhere but at home."

TENNIS

Milan had decided to compete in an international tennis tournament held in Prague, even though he would be five years older at least than his nearest competitor, and moreover the tournament was intended for young talent hoping to turn professional on the strength of their performance. Nothing in the paperwork said that Milan was ineligible, although he did expect to get knocked out in the first round. I wanted to stay to watch, but my mom had already booked return tickets, and I felt that I was a failure as a friend and teacher and a witness to Milan's story.

Hundreds of parents, dozens of coaches, and scores of hopefuls descended on Prague, and in many, most, or all cases, spent more than the $10,000 prize money on training, hotels, food, and tickets. Ivan e-mailed that he noticed in the sports pages of his newspaper that there was some grumbling about a local man, older, described variously as grumpy and savage, progressing through the tournament, and evidently shattering dreams and aborting careers in the process. The Czechs were proud to see their colors honored, but it was universally agreed that the man's style of play was disturbing, and amounted to a form of psychological warfare that disconcerted each opponent's every move. Stronger, faster, nimbler, sprier opponents were systematically dispatched.

Milan did not claim the prize, although he reached the quarterfinals, which he lost in straight sets to a nineteen-year-old from Japan. Back home in Indiana, I watched it on TV. I knew nothing about tennis, but Milan had told me that he served at 120 miles per hour, and it looked to me as though he didn't need to do much more than that. His black shorts and shirt bore no logo, his shoes were black, and his racket had no design on the face that I could make out; he was a man out of patience with the pieties and proprieties of tennis.

In play he was powerful with moments of grace but nothing of flair or style; he was like a hulking backwoodsman with a claymore swinging at some effete rapier-wielding metropolitan. When he served or returned he did so convincingly, and sometimes unanswerably, and he was not slow, but he expended tremendous energy with every swing of his racket and held nothing back to respond or persevere with. In the third set I could hear his breathing even over the airwaves, as I watched him succumb not so much to his adversary as his own age, lack of training, and inefficiency.

Yet I saw why he had made the papers, and why he had made the quarterfinals. Whenever the ball was not in play he studied his racket, rapt and oblivious, caressing the handle or touching the strings, lost in interstitial mysteries: as though his racket were really a mirror, and the mirror posed an overwhelming question. His serve was what necessarily followed when he tossed the question lightly into the air.

EPILOGUE

Years later, when I had the best job title of anyone I knew—sommelier—I was invited to visit Moravia at the end of a week spent evaluating Rieslings in the Mosel and writing my impressions for a trade magazine. I had been married, then divorced, and I lived in Nova Scotia after stints in Colorado and California. My parents still lived in Indiana, where I had worked my way conventionally up from waiter to shift manager to wine steward with a certification earned at a three-week course in St. Louis. Even then it took years for me to look old enough to be trusted. In any case the job had always consisted of about ninety percent making decent conversation. I discovered by accident that if I grew a beard, two entirely white tufts emerged on either side of my chin. I was told that I looked like I belonged on a horse. From that point on I was an asset to any restaurant with pretentions.

I hadn't really thought of Amanda for years until one day in a steep-sloped German vineyard, when I was following the winemaker, who had introduced police goats to arrest criminal weeds and deter hooligan birds, up to a favorite ledge of his for a panoramic view of his domain. It occurred to me that if one of those goats disliked a person that person might tumble a long way vertically and fail to wake up. I stared too long into one goat's eyes and began to doubt my own self-worth. Perhaps our balcony neighbor had experienced something similar with one of his pigeons.

I asked the winemaker—a tall jovial man in his fifties named Thorsten—if he had ever been to Prague. I was planning to follow through with questions about Moravian wines, because I was sure his opinions would be more charitable than mine, and I could later borrow them. Winemakers crave praise like children crave attention.

He said that in his opinion, Prague, like Paris, was no longer worth visiting: plagued by tourists, horrifically expensive, with exactly the same standards of food and service you would expect in any other major city; there was nothing you could get in Prague that you couldn't get from the Internet. Some smaller cities and towns remained Czech and charming, and I should visit Krumlov or Brno instead. Prague was like a giant hotel or cruise ship affixed to an airport overdue for expansion.

A nearby goat dismantled some pretty pink wildflowers. Thorsten waved his hand over his perfect placid slopes and said I could spend my week there instead if I liked. A week of Moravian wines might damage my palate irreparably.

As I rolled through Germany on the train I considered time-of-life questions that never troubled me and Amanda: the age and development of children, interest rates paid and years outstanding on a mortgage, career advancement; each of those had impinged on subsequent relationships, and I began to think of the station names that slid past as former lovers, as though I had once been devoted to Lukavec, Keblice, Rochov, and Doksany—lovely and languid with naked laps covered in petals of wildflowers. By the time we arrived at the main station in Prague the train wheels were repeating her name: Amanda, Amanda, Amanda. I could never tell whether she became herself or became who she thought she was expected to be, or whether there was any real difference.

The station convulsed with young people in bright athletic gear, and the street outside was a menacing shoal of sleek new cars. The elderly and otherwise unsightly had all been banished; health, wealth, and sex were promised from every vertical surface adequate to hold an advertisement, unless it was a historical surface advertising itself. The only obvious distinction between residents and tourists was that the former group talked into their phones while the latter took selfies. I'd have loved to stop for a beer but not on Western terms of satisfaction or contentment. I had only my carry-on luggage so I walked to my hotel within shouting distance of Graceland.

A receptionist with flawless English showed me to my room on the fourth floor, and it was immaculate, like a prison cell from IKEA. One window looked over a courtyard, but the window was locked and the courtyard was a restaurant garden with trellises and fairy lights and wall decorations at head level and people sampling tapas on tables while sitting in chairs. Somehow I hadn't known that something so mundane could be so painful to look at.

I was still in touch with some of my students. Ivan lived in Annecy and worked in Geneva with an hour's drive each way that did terrible things to his back. Cimarron lived in Stockholm, where he had grown a beard to confuse predators, and had returned to carpentry. I had lost touch with Vlasta, and Milan when last heard from was deep in the Bohemian countryside attempting to finish writing a novel. It seemed that I no longer knew anybody in Prague, or if I did I was uncertain how to reach them.

Somehow Amanda and I had failed to make or to keep mutual friends. My attempts at contacting her had petered out years before, and it was impossible to go through every Facebook profile under her name. It occurred to me, aimlessly wandering tiny alleys, as alien to me as they were when I first wandered them with Amanda, that perhaps I could by some juxtaposition of guess and memory find the door to the Radovans' flat. The Sex Machines Museum indicated a likely area, but the baroque architecture there suggested a youthfulness that the Radovans' building did not share. A gate of undressed stone seemed promising, and on the other side every façade tilted into or away from the street like toys dropped by a child or teeth in need of a dentist. Light pooled timidly under streetlamps and cobblestones moved underfoot. Fleetingly I thought I was back in Real Prague—that Real Prague still existed—but I had merely stumbled into another film set, or so I inferred from a wooden signpost indicating directions to Cambridge and Oxford.

When I did find the door to the Radovans' flat there was no longer a forty-foot brunette in a black leather bra presiding over the façade opposite, or any sign of a strip club. I pressed the buzzer. Mrs. Radovan's voice answered through the doorside speaker, in Czech. When I persuaded her to speak English she couldn't remember who I was. When I mentioned Amanda Mrs. Radovan buzzed me in.

The flat looked shabbier than it had, with dust on shelves

and cigarette burns in the sofa, and though Mrs. Radovan had not visibly aged much to my eye her movements were slower and her voice less effusive, and she told me immediately that Radovan had died three years previously: an ischemic stroke followed by double pneumonia; but, she said, he had gone swiftly and painlessly before he really fell apart. She did not rate herself a very good widow. His violin and bow still hung on the living room wall above a record player flanked by what must have been a historically significant record collection.

She remembered me by sight, she said, and apologized for not remembering my name. I was most welcome to a glass of wine.

The prodigal son had returned for his father's funeral, and had switched his mobile phone off for exactly the length of the service, then declined to stay overnight. More than a few Swiss girls, she added, had had more than enough of him. I could see that Mrs. Radovan's dissatisfactions were legion.

Mrs. Radovan thought it splendid that I worked in wine. Knowing the *histoire* of a terroir and appreciating its fruit was the job of a real historian, she said, and it was good that I had not become a scholar buried alive in some archive. It was a special thing to divine the provenance of an organic thing in a world of synthetic garbage, to understand the mere contingencies of which all things ultimately consist, to grasp equations rather than algorithms, whereby terrain and time and weather and labor yielded a unique value also confined by time and circumstance and the unique characteristics of an individual's palate and sensibilities. In that line lay everything. I thought she was overstating the case.

I expected her to ask me how Amanda was doing, but instead she told me. Amanda had visited Prague within the past twelve months, and had visited once before that, too, when Radovan was still alive.

On the most recent visit Amanda had brought an infant girl, named Lily May after a boat her mother had seen a week before Amanda was due. The child was sixteen or eighteen months old at the time, screamed on public transport, rarely slept, and hated food, even Mrs. Radovan's. Amanda had not, she said, looked good. On the previous visit Amanda had traveled with a man Mrs. Radovan later presumed to be the child's father.

She paused to ask if I would like more merlot, and I assented.

Mrs. Radovan and her husband had both sensed trouble on that earlier visit. Amanda's companion was handsome, courteous, older, and employed as the commander of a destroyer in the Royal Navy or some such dashing thing. But his manner, said Mrs. Radovan—the way he touched things like books and forks like he was mad at them—augured ill, and the umbrage he took at Radovan's jokes at his expense would have got him evicted had he not been Amanda's guest. Mrs. Radovan said, in perfect sincerity, that she did not understand couples who fight, as she and her husband had done so very seldomly, and while she was talking I became absurdly overwhelmed by a feeling of moral responsibility for and toward a little English girl named after a boat.

Mrs. Radovan began to yawn and I began to fret about the etiquette of keeping an old widow awake past her bedtime. She insisted that I stay for one more drink, and I thought that was the most human beings should ever expect from each other anyway. Mrs. Radovan's wine was the only real thing and Mrs. Radovan and I the only real people in Prague just then. Smetana looked as though Dvořák had just pinched his ear. The great black fireplace was a gilded theater, the violin opposite

Smetana gleamed on the wall. Mrs. Radovan laughed at my jokes for some reason, while I got immersed in her stories—how dashing the SS men were and how courteous the Nazi officers handing out chocolates to Czech children in 1938, and how poorly the smelly spotty Russian boys of 1968 stood up to comparison.

I left the room to use the toilet and when I returned I thought Mrs. Radovan had been attacked. She slumped halfway along the sofa, eyes closed, mouth open, as if she had been toppled there by some unseen but powerful force. I moved closer to check if she was still breathing, but it occurred to me that whatever had assaulted her must still be in the room. I looked over my shoulder and saw nothing but felt exposed: as if the nothing that was not there would be something sometime, and the room though perfectly empty and quiet seethed with thieves and informants and murderers and madmen, each of them assailed and animated themselves by demons and maladies, stretching from that room to the next to the next through all of Prague and all of Bohemia and beyond Bavaria and from Mount Fuji to the Golden Gate Bridge and across and throughout and beyond time.

I could see her shoulders moving, I thought, so I began instead to think about what I knew of symptoms of strokes or heart attacks—nothing—and whether there were particular tricks and skills for dealing with the elderly, or if there were things a trained eye would look for. I decided to try shaking her shoulder gently, but as I edged around the coffee table she issued a tremendous snort.

I stood still watching as she slowly exhaled, and grew mesmerized by a thin strand of saliva dangling from the corner of her mouth. Her next stallionesque inhalation broke the spell, and I sat down. As she settled more deeply into sleep, the rhythm of her snoring suggested some esoteric industrial machinery grinding out items of obscure purpose. It seemed wrong to wake her up.

She woke me at around 3:30, because I had drifted off in my chair. I had a recurring dream of a beautiful city covered in mud, and all the residents blamed me for putting it there. In this dream Amanda slid past laughing, because that was what mud was for. Yet whichever way I turned, the only way was uphill. Mrs. Radovan said I could take the sofa if I liked but that she needed to get to her bed. We each said farewell in Czech and I stepped out the door and downstairs.

Outside the air was pristine and cool, and the streets empty, as though I had arrived the moment after everyone was summoned to the Last Judgment. I didn't go straight back to my room. I just walked around by myself, waiting for sunlight to make everything bright and clean and new.

ACKNOWLEDGMENTS

Děkuji moc for many reasons to Tim O'Connell, Mary-Anne Harrington, Anna Kaufman, Will Francis, Margaret and Clark Kimberling, and Sandra Niedersberg.

Na zdraví to Andreea Petre-Goncalves, Carolyn Baugh, Shefali Malhoutra, Hana Komanová, Šárka Tobrmanová-Kühnová, Lola Estelle, Phil Rose, Joanne Dexter, Sean Connolly, Denis Fourré, and Géraldine Carvello.

Brian Kimberling grew up in southern Indiana and spent two years working in the Czech Republic, Mexico, and Turkey before settling in England. He received an MA in creative writing from Bath Spa University in 2010, and his first novel, *Snapper,* was published in 2013.

A NOTE ON THE TYPE

This book was set in Adobe Garamond. Designed for the Adobe Corporation by Robert Slimbach, the fonts are based on types first cut by Claude Garamond (c. 1480–1561). It is to him that we owe the letter we now know as "old style."

Typeset by Scribe, Philadelphia, Pennsylvania
Printed and bound by Berryville Graphics, Berryville, Virginia
Designed by Maggie Hinders